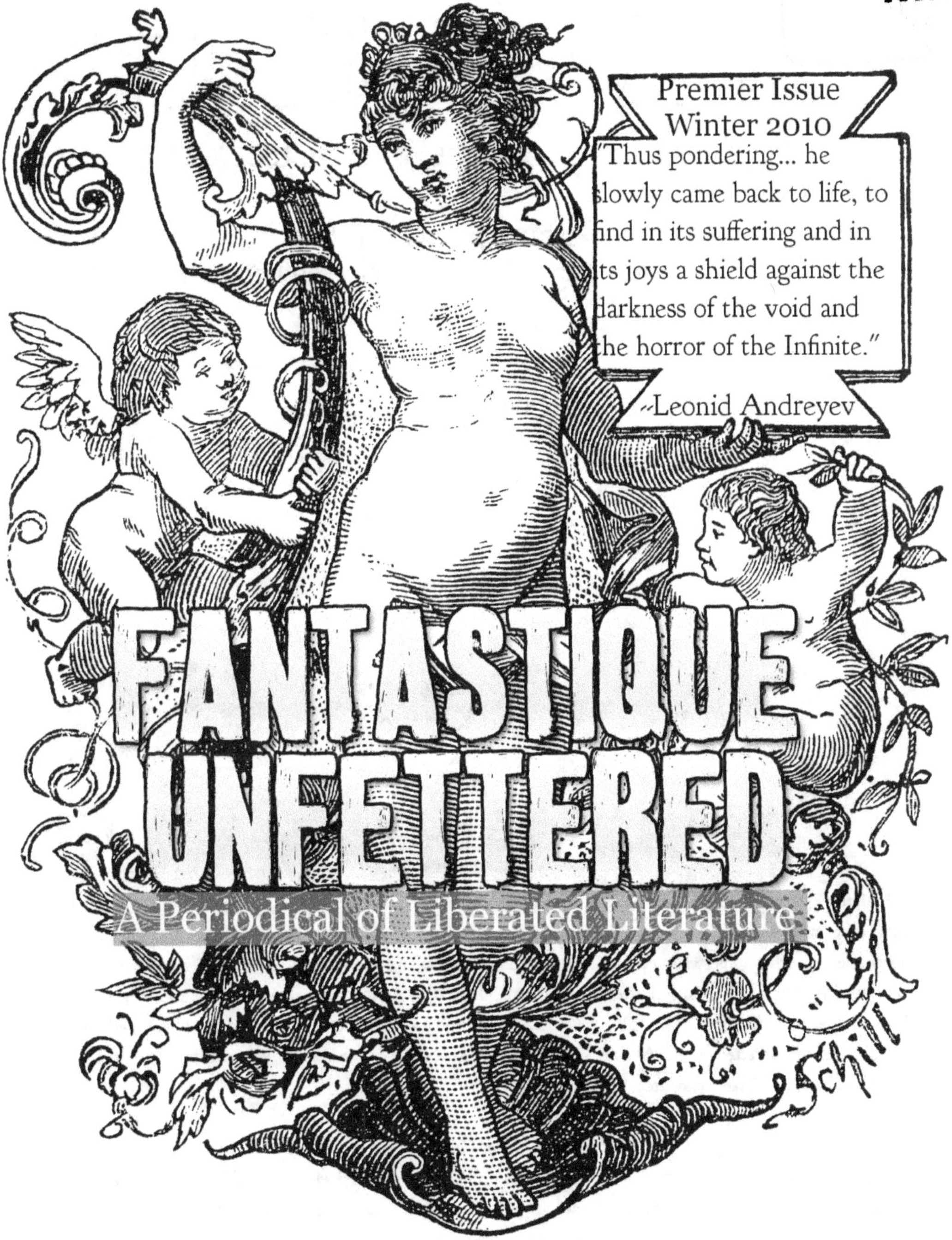
Premier Issue
Winter 2010
"Thus pondering... he slowly came back to life, to find in its suffering and in its joys a shield against the darkness of the void and the horror of the Infinite."
-Leonid Andreyev
FANTASTIQUE UNFETTERED
A Periodical of Liberated Literature
Schill

FANTASTIQUE UNFETTERED

A Periodical of Liberated Literature

An M-Brane Press Publication
Publisher   Christopher Fletcher

Editor
Brandon H. Bell

Art & Design Consultant
M. S. Corley

Slush, Editorial Assts.
William Wood, Jaym Gates

Contributing Artist
Mari Kurisato

Thoughts on (Kalpa)...

Two of my daughters are named after writers whose work I read when I was a teenager. Ellison, Delany. Stories hold meaning for me that I've struggled to express in this introduction. Ellison in particular wrote a passage that asked what it was like when the first Neanderthal crouched on a ledge and realized he was the last. I've not found that passage to properly quote it: thought it in Angry Candy, but memory may deceive. To my younger self, these words told me I wasn't alone. Someone else out there understood.

The anguish that looms large as a kid can seem trivial as an adult. Ours is a world of great anguish, fear, cruelty: what are our petty sufferings against a history of suffering?

And, still, our writers tell their tales. Cast them out into history to add their voices to the great chorus of our imagining. Words, words, words.

That, maybe, someone else will hear and know themselves not alone. Or, short of that, to find distraction in a tale well told.

From the depths of pre-history, storytellers have sat about fires and whispered stories for these reasons and more. Those stories propagated among listeners, became myth, culture, archetype. No one owned those stories. Everyone owned those stories.

We believe creators should make money at their craft (and we'd like your support so that we can pay our creators more) AND we believe no one should own our culture. FU's basic concept, the 'unfettered' part of our name, is nothing new: it is old as the oldest of stories.

So, herein, a contribution to the kalpas. Please enjoy.

~Brandon H. Bell, Nov. 28th, 2010

Contents

Premier Issue | Winter 2010

Editorial Content

Poetry

Fiction

About FU

Boris

by

Annam Manthiram

Herein, messages received may be heeded, ignored, or misunderstood.

Lovelle likes to take off everything. One moment, she is fully-clothed; the next, she is a dry ghost in need of lotion. Sarita, my wife, prefers to unravel herself in front of my judging eyes, much like a ball of yarn. Perhaps this is something she has learned from watching Bollywood porn.

Lovelle smells of rice flour and smoke derived from Gitane cigarettes. Sarita smells of jasmine and burritos stuffed with cumin. When I am with one, I think of the other. When I am asleep, I think of a third, but I am unsure yet who the third will be. But I am certain that there will be a third.

I am in the bathroom. The water is running in the sink. I examine the tag on my shirt. It reads, "Made in Colombia. Do Not Eat Today." I put on my glasses and read it again. The tag reads the same. I place the tag under water, and the words seem abnormally large against my small, weak hands. It does not wash away like I want.

"Lovelle, please come read this," I ask. She slithers out of bed, the way one would imagine a snail leaving its shell if it must. She comes to the bathroom and leans her head against the door frame, her bright red hair offering (sometimes) a much needed distraction from her face.

"What is it, darling? I am not in the mood for it in the bathroom." Her voice is unnaturally saucy, sans cherry. She leans over the sink, and I feel one of her nipples grazing my arm, the way a dog grazes a piece of hotdog. I shake it off as I will come to shake off Sarita's "I'm home" kiss.

"Can you read this tag?" I ask.

"No," she says. She flips her hair and it catches me in the eye. If she could, she would exist as a bubble, allowing the world to see her, but not touching or changing the world in any way. But she cannot. Ugliness is attractive. My wife doesn't understand that.

"Please, Lovelle, it's important to me." The ugly also wield power. Many of them don't know this yet, but she does.

Lovelle does not answer, but goes back to my bed. She looks like a snow angel, but without the snow and without the look of innocence.

I begin to go through the rest of my closet. I find an old corduroy shirt that Sarita gave me for a birthday. She always gifts me with shirts. I loathe her lack of creativity, but also appreciate her predictable nature. Comfort can be found in patterns. I know this year that she will get me a linen shirt; she is making her way through the fabric rainbow. Next year will be flannel.

I take the corduroy shirt off its hanger and examine the label. It reads, "Made in the USA. Hand and Fist Are Not the Same." I look at my hand, and then I look at it again as a fist. Sarita doesn't sew. Neither does Lovelle. I've always wanted to be with a seamstress. I imagine her nimble fingers rubbing my body at equal intervals, the way a carefully placed stitch appears on a shirt sleeve. Perhaps she will be my third.

"Lovelle, where is your blouse?"

"Boris, when are you going to leave your wife?"

When she doesn't want to answer a question of mine, she responds with a question of her own. Most often, they are questions about my wife. When are you going to kiss her again? Do you think of me when you are with her? Does she wash her behind the way you do? Neither of us gets the answer we desire, but I am not so sure we are looking for an answer.

"Please don't call me Boris." I prefer people to call me "mister," "sir," or any other masculine term of anonymity. I was born with a name that people often mistake for being European. When I introduce myself, they are confused, but it isn't difficult to confuse most people. Confusion leads to questions, intruding ones. I find by smiling and showing people my crooked teeth, they usually go away. Who said smiling was the universal symbol of friendship? Perhaps a dentist.

I crawl underneath the bed and find her blouse. Today she has worn the white one with the pink hearts on the bosom. She knows I cannot tolerate the shirt. Sarita's favorite color is white, and early on, before I caught on to Lovelle's manipulations, I had answered her question about Sarita's preferred color of choice. Now, I cannot get Lovelle to stop wearing the saintly shade. Being with her feels as though I am with an Indian widow. The association at first turned me on, but now it makes me tired.

I read the tag, and it says, "Made in India. Leave Her Now."

"Wake up, please," I whine. I hate to be so obsequious, especially with someone as ugly as she is, but I have learned that that is the only way to get a response from her. She has already fallen asleep, another characteristic I despise in her. She dreams as soon as her head touches the pillow. I must count sheep. Lately I've been counting

A woman with artwork on her body should know something about taking lovers.

9

the number of women I've slept with since I've come to this country.

I stare at her and shake her bottom as though I am fluffing a sofa cushion. I wonder sometimes if she can detect my contempt for her. I cannot get away though. She is oddly in control of the relationship, although I am the one who laid claim to her first. Her careless and at times indifferent attitude toward me and life in general is intoxicating. I want to make her like life more. Perhaps that is why I stay, but I am a man after all. I probably stay because she is free and easy to maintain, unlike the plants that my wife keeps in the house.

"What is it, sir?" She itches at her eyes, and I see that they already have sleep in them.

"Come," I say. I pull off her underwear, and she coos like a pigeon trapped in the palm of my hand.

"I will at this rate," she says. I push her away from my face. I turn the tag over on her panties, and it reads, "Made in China. Not Free."

I realize that I need to get away from her to think. My favorite place to meditate is in the laundry room of the basement of my apartment building. The drone of the ancient machines reminds me of a prehistoric time. I imagine the only sounds the cavemen heard were each other's animalistic screams and the thunder in the sky.

When I sit on the dryer, I close my eyes and I can transcend to that place, where women were not complicated and men got what they wanted when they wanted.

As I close the door, I see Lovelle's face buried in my favorite pillow. She doesn't drool, but my picture of her would almost be better if she did. When I get to the basement, I find that both machines are occupied. On top of the washing machine, someone has left her laundry basket. It is pink, not unlike the parts of Lovelle that I do really love. Out of curiosity, I open the lid and take out a scalloped bra. It is a 32A, and I know I have never seen any woman as small as that in my building before.

I sit and wait for the petite woman in the laundry room, certain that she will provide me with some sort of guidance. They rarely ever disappoint me. My best friend is a Napoleon figure. He is an asshole, but clever as a deceptive Leprechaun. This new woman will tell me if I am delusional and if Lovelle is the ugliest woman she's ever seen, first to my own wife. I could start an army of the women I've fucked: the ugly army.

Burfi finally arrives. I am not sure of her name, but that is what I think of when I see her – a coconut dessert bar topped with flakes of sugar and pistachio nuts.

"Burfi, you're finally here," I say.

"Sebastian?" She asks. She too has

sleep in her eyes.

"Who's Sebastian? Is that your father?" She looks young enough to still have a father. My wife's father died from complications related to diabetes, bloated on sugar cane juice given to him by his malicious servants in India. Lovelle's father abused her as a child; so she'd emancipated herself at age 16 and never returned. I heard the same story from so many women I couldn't even be empathic anymore. I felt like a bad person, but emotions dull over time.

"Sorry, you looked like someone I knew once. That I had met online."

"Online?"

"Never mind."

We stand in silence, I admiring the carpet of tattoos that cover her body.

"Should I acquire a third or get rid of one?" I ask her. A woman with artwork on her body should know something about taking lovers.

"I don't know what you're talking about."

"Women."

She takes a second as if debating with herself on whether to answer. "Do they know about each other?"

"No, why would they?"

"Are they beautiful?"

"No. I don't think so. But beautiful women – they cost more." I remember the bus conductor in Chennai, back when the city was still called Madras and back when I was still in college with no driver and no bicycle. The only solace was Radha, the bus lady; her name suited her perfectly. I could've traced her figure in circles only; she was that geometric. When men tried to make advances at her or whistle, she'd flirt with them, collecting their names and addresses and promising to pay a visit. Then, at least how the rumor went, she'd send her brothers – all five of them like the mythical Pandavas from the Mahabharata – and assault the perverts.

"Are they nice people?"

"What does that have to do with it?" I ask.

"Don't you care if you hurt their feelings?"

"Oh no. They have been through far worse. I could never hurt them the way they have already been hurt. They are impenetrable." Sometimes I want to though, but I know especially with Lovelle, I cannot. She is much too strong for me. Sarita would just beat me with a deep fryer.

She stops talking, and I know I have offended her. I used to care, but I don't anymore. I stare at her, hoping to provoke her into a response or some sort of outburst, but she holds her calm. After the dryer makes a beep, she collects her belongings and scatters. I find that she has left the bra behind. Before I tuck it inside my shirt, I read the tag. It says, "Made in Honduras.

Listen."

When I return to my apartment, Lovelle is missing. My wife has left a message on the answering machine. It says, "I'm ovulating." Her syrupy voice gives me the chills. I said yes to her demands because the miscarriage rate is nearly 13%. I have always been good with odds.

Lovelle returns with her arms filled with paper sacks of flour and greased newspaper covering tins of freshly churned butter.

"I'm going to make you a cake, sir," she says, scooping out the flour with her bare hands.

"What is the occasion?"

"Life," she says, and I know she has heard the message.

"I love you, Lovelle," I say, hoping to distract her. I don't believe that I am really in love with her, but she knows that we sometimes must play these games, where I am the devoted boyfriend and she is the beautiful girlfriend. Smart men wouldn't waste their energies on affairs; they'd tackle the world's problems instead. Unfortunately, as social creatures, we cannot escape the habits of lesser men.

"Oh, sir," she says. She smears flour on her bottom and shakes it in front of my face as though rattling a toy in front of a small child. She whips the batter into a frothy yellow cream and pours it into delicate aluminum cups. She sticks the tray into the oven, and I realize that my oven has been on all night.

"Come eat," she says.

"They are not ready, you just put them in the oven." She places her pinky finger onto my lips and quiets me with her coral-colored eyes. She has a paper bag, and from inside she produces a perfect slice of chocolate cake.

"For me?" I ask. My stomach gurgles the way my car sometimes does after a tune-up. I grab Lovelle and start to make love to her among the dirty dishes. My wife will be home soon.

"Boris, eat your cake!" She screams the way she does when I have done something good. That is so very rare with her. I take the cake and eat it with my hands. My mother always used to scold me for eating with my fingers even though that's what Indians do. We were Indians trying to be British back then, but even she couldn't stop me now. She was dead.

"I am sleepy, Lovelle. Will you come rest with me?" My full stomach has made me tired. I hear the key turn in the lock. Sarita already?

"Lovelle?" She just smiles and closes her eyes. I force myself awake and see Sarita enter the apartment. The two women smile at each other, and before I drift to sleep, I read the tag on her shirt again. It says, "Good Night." I try to reach for Lovelle's hand, and then Sarita's, but I cannot find them.

Instead, I can hear them laughing, both voices so loud that I cover my ears and drown myself in sound.

Annam Manthiram is the author of two novels, *The Goju Story* and *After the Tsunami*, and a short story collection (*Dysfunction*), which was a Finalist in the 2010 Elixir Press Fiction Award and received Honorable Mention in Leapfrog Press' 2010 fiction contest. Annam's fiction has also been nominated for the PEN/O'Henry Prize and inclusion in the Best American Short Stories anthology. A graduate of the M.A. Writing program at the University of Southern California and a 2010 Squaw Valley Writers Conference scholar, Ms. Manthiram resides in New Mexico with her husband, Alex, and son, Sathya. So far, she is quite enchanted. You can visit her online at **AnnamManthiram.com**.

Without a Light

by

Natania Barron

Herein, dear reader, one is obliged to find not love or romance, but desire, and darkness, and whispers.

Clint knew better than to argue with Principal Czysky. She peered at him over her tinted and bejeweled glasses, the gold scrollwork glinting as she moved her head through the shadows and light cast on her desk. Clint could never tell what color her eyes were with those glasses, and it unsettled him almost as much as her fuzzy, cat-hair covered sweaters.

Czysky tapped her purple fingernails on the Formica desk and shook her head. Even with such a motion her hair didn't move; it had been Aqua-netted and frosted into a teased helmet of curls that defied any attempt at disarray.

"Let me try this again, Clint. Do you know how many parent complaints I've had this week?" she asked.

Clint didn't know. He shrugged and tried to care.

"Six," finished Czysky, holding up one splayed hand, and then an index finger. Clint sensed an implied middle-finger salute.

"Well," Clint said, pulling on the cuff of his tweed jacket. Although he'd never worn anything like it at Ashuelot Middle School in the Berkshires, where he'd taught for three years after college, he had hoped the more professional appearance might endear him to Czysky and the Board. "You don't think they're just having a difficult time adjusting to a new teacher? I mean, I know Mr. Barnes—"

Czysky narrowed her eyes. "Clinton," she said. Not even his mother had called him Clinton. "Mr. Barnes was adored. You've got big shoes to fill. But Mr. Barnes also didn't tell his sixth grade class that the Civil War had nothing to do with slavery."

"Mrs.—"

"Listen. I don't care what you learned in that hippie liberal shit-hole of a college you went to," she said, leaning over her desk. The braided gold chain she wore on her neck swung forward, its cluster of heart-shaped charms scraping across the desk. "You teach my kids about the *slaves*, about Harriet *Tubman*, about the Underground Railroad, and give them some good old fashioned Negro spirituals to learn. 'Follow the Drinking Gourd' is always a good one. That's what Mr. Barnes did, and that's what the parents expect."

"Jesus," Clint said, leaning back in his chair as she leaned forward. "I was just trying to give them another perspective."

"They're in the *sixth grade*. They only need one perspective. The one in the book."

"My sixth graders at Ashuelot—"

"Your sixth graders were in a middle school," Czysky interrupted. "A drug-infested, *liberal*, horrifying place where, if I recall, two summers ago three sixth graders committed suicide. We keep our sixth graders here, at Blackfield Elementary, to protect them and prepare them for Blackfield Academy."

Blackfield Academy was the fancy name for the ugly brick building where 7th-12th grade resided, to the tune of 220 souls. Blackfield itself had just under 4,000 residents as it was.

"Yes, ma'am, I understand," Clint said. He only needed to comply. As he spoke the words he heard her relax into her shoulder-pads.

"Still. I'm putting you on probation."

"Probation?" he asked. "From what?"

"I'm requiring you to attend faculty lunches. I expect you to be at lunch every day for the next two weeks. And soccer tryouts are next week."

"Soccer?"

"You said in your application and interview that you were a sports fan."

"Fan being the operative term."

"You'll do fine. They're just kids, after all."

—

Clint knew there was no way in hell he'd seen her before, because a pair of legs like that would never have passed his notice. Not to mention her ass. She was dressed smartly, in a beige suit jacket and matching short skirt; she had a purple scarf tied around her neck, and her corn silk blond hair curled just at the ends.

When she caught his eye, Clint noticed how dark her eyes were.

"Oh, hi," she said, stopping short. She had a brown paper bag in her hand and was, Clint noticed with a grin, heading toward the teacher's lounge. "I'm sorry—I almost walked straight into you."

"No problem," he said. "I'm Clint—Mr. Apwood, by the way. I don't think we've met yet."

Clint felt the unfamiliar flush of embarrassment. He had not considered that she knew the lengths to which he'd gone to find out about her. He'd thought he'd outsmarted her.

"Ah, the new Mr. Barnes," she replied with a smile. Her teeth were not straight, but it was cute. "I'm Emily Stevens. Ms. Stevens. First Grade. I've been away at a conference since of my students is special needs," she said, as politely as she could. "Mrs. Czysky wanted me to get some certification. I went all the way to Boston, and now I'm behind on all my planning, and all I want is a cigarette."

"Don't have any?"

"Trying to quit."

He pulled out his Winstons. "Be my guest. If you want."

Emily lowered her voice, "Oh, shit yes." She took a cigarette and looked left and right. "Want to come with?"

Clint chuckled as he followed Emily through a set of double doors and into a little alcove facing the soccer field; he felt like a rebellious teenager skipping class.

"You said you we're trying to quit," he said, watching her drag lovingly on the cigarette and then let the smoke linger in her mouth before expelling; a seasoned smoker.

"Jesus, if only this were weed," she said, tossing her hair back with the practiced air of a high school cheerleader. She had the build for it.

He couldn't help but laugh this time. "Well, maybe next time."

"Nah, we don't want to incur the wrath of Czysky the Bedazzled Beast."

"Czysky? Yeah, she called my college a shit-hole," Clint said. "And I think she might that the word 'liberal' is a swear."

Emily grinned again, then stubbed out her cigarette with her boot-heel. She wiggled her fingers, and Clint complied, turning over another one without question. The woman had power. He liked it.

"Yeah, but, that's how they are here. They treat anyone who's not geriatric like they're threats because we've got more education between us than half the staff put together. Presuming you have a degree in education?"

"Masters," said Clint, automatically.

"Fancy."

"So how did you end up in Blackfield?"

"I taught in the Berkshires. It wasn't so bad. A little weird at times, but you know."

"I bet it's nowhere near as weird as here," Emily said, shaking her head. She glanced at her watch.

Clint looked across the soccer field to the neat row of houses in the distance. They were all two-story colonials, with closed-in porches, matching siding of varying shades of yellow. Most had contrasting dark shutters in brown. It was warm enough, being September, but the trees were already starting to shift from green to crisp gold and orange.

"Oh, Jesus," Emily said. She wheeled

around, throwing her cigarette at the same time. "Walter, what are you doing out here?"

"What is it?" Clint asked, half expecting to see a lumbering boyfriend or incensed groundskeeper.

A little boy stood with his hands over his ears, just a few paces to their right. How he escaped from lunch, he had no idea. Walter was pudgy, wearing a striped shirt and trousers with tennis shoes. His eyes were round, blue or green, but someone had taken care to part his hair just so. It made him look like a middle-aged salesman.

"Walter—you're not supposed to leave lunch," Emily said, walking to him and crouching down, staring into his face.

She sighed, then leaned over and kissed Walter on the cheek. It lasted much longer than Clint wanted it to, and he turned away feeling his stomach squirm.

When he looked back again, Emily was standing, her hand on Walter's head—a protective stance. Everything about her posture and presence had shifted.

The bell rang.

"Well—" Clint started.

"Yes... this is Walter," Emily said. "He's my special boy." She smiled with her lips, and turned to take Walter back to his class.

Clint stood a while, catching his breath, watching his cigarette smolder between his fingers.

—

"Nah, it's nothing serious," Clint said on a call with his brother Wayne. It was late, but Wayne and Vasco were on Pacific time. Clint knew he should be sleeping, but since meeting Emily Stevens, he was restless. "She just bums cigarettes from me at this point."

"That's where it starts," Wayne said, chuckling into the receiver. Clint could hear yapping in the background, and Vasco shouting at the dogs.

Clint stared out across the street from the window at his kitchen table. The streetlight illuminated the jagged shapes of all the shit that the neighbors across the street had dumped into their yard. He had a mind to complain one of these days.

"Knowing you, it'll take a week," Wayne said.

"She's not that kind of girl. I mean, she's very career-oriented."

"So she doesn't fake it like you?"

Clint snorted.

Wayne was giggling. "You're intimidated by her smarts?"

"I just don't know how she can work here. It's a vacuum of closed-mindedness. I just..."

"She's a *challenge*, you mean," Wayne said. "You've been working on her how long?"

Clint counted back the days. "Eight days, total. Not counting weekends."

"Shit, Clint. Then she's taken. Doesn't mean there's no hope, but just make sure she's not dating a linebacker, okay? I'm not there to prevent you from getting beaten up."

"You never—"

There was a scuffle of dogs, and more screaming from Vasco.

"Shit, I gotta go. Darlene just shit on the carpet." Darlene was the oldest of the dogs, and the matriarch of the pack. "Call you later, bro. Good luck."

Wayne hung up, and Clint continued to look out the window into the darkness. Moths gathered at the streetlight for one of the last times before it got too cold. It was going to start frosting again soon.

—

Clint sat closest to the door at lunch, but he hadn't spotted her yet. It had been three lunches since she had last bummed a cigarette from him, and he had the pack within easy reach of his hands, just so.

Women never unsettled him as she did, but he hadn't been with a woman since Nancy at Ashuelot. Hell, since meeting Emily Clint had started smoking more.

Finally he saw the swoosh of a gray skirt, the edge of her heels, the ends of her hair. She was talking to someone outside of the frame of the door, and let out a forced laugh. Dipping into the doorframe she widened her eyes at him and wiggled her fingers.

When they got outside it was drizzling.

"God, what a day," Emily said, taking the cigarette before Clint had fully extended his arm.

He fumbled for his lighter, and when the cigarette was finally lit she inhaled angrily, half spitting out the smoke.

"You okay?" he asked.

"This fucking school," she hissed, brushing her thin fingers across her brow, pausing a moment to massage the bridge of her nose.

"Hey, I was thinking... wanna go out for a beer after—"

He didn't even get the whole sentence out before she interrupted.

"No," she said, firmly, putting her hand on his wrist. Her fingers were colder than the air. And he'd pissed her off. "It's just no." She ground out the cigarette on the brick, and went back inside.

Clint crumpled the essay and closed his eyes. The headache had started an hour ago and, in spite of the ibuprofen and coffee and scotch, had only intensified to the point that the letters on the page were rimmed in red.

More scotch. He'd risk the hangover tomorrow if it meant getting rid of the throbbing in his head.

Glancing out the window he noticed there were no more moths at the streetlight, but there was--

"Well, fuck me," he said.

It was Emily Stevens.

When he came within speaking distance—he had to go around the house to get to the streetlamp as his apartment didn't have street access—she had already started to walk away, her black and white checked scarf fluttering behind her.

"Emily!" he called. "Hey, wait up a sec."

She stopped, her arms flopping down by her side as if in defeat.

"Come on. It's freezing out here."

"I really..." she trailed off, turning around slowly. She looked perfect in the lamplight, her pale hair shot with gold, her lips flushed red. So red.

"I've got nothing to offer you but Sanka, so I won't take it personally if you go somewhere else."

That elicited a sliver of a smile. "Fine. But just for a few minutes. I can't feel my feet."

Clint was painfully aware of the slovenly state of his apartment as he ushered Emily in. He wished he'd at least taken out the garbage. Somehow the pervasive stench of the trashcan was even worse after having been outside in the clean, cold air.

He had to move a stack of papers out of her way to allow enough space for both of them at his kitchen table. And really, table was too kind a word. It was more of an elongated tray that had not seen a dust-rag since he moved in, stuck with bits of crumbs and more than its share of rings from beer bottles.

If she was unsettled, however, she made no indication. Emily tucked her hands under her armpits and waited silently as Clint put the kettle on and rummaged for the sugar. He had a splash of milk left in the jug.

"You take cream or milk or—"

"It's Sanka. It's not like adding stuff to it will improve the taste."

"Yeah. Sorry about that." He leaned back against the counter top, the cool metal edge pressing into his back and through his t-shirt. The whole kitchen was a blue and silver throwback to the 50s and had a certain hermetic charm to it.

He cleared his throat under her

stare. She didn't blink much. "You live around here, then?"

"No, not really. Close to the school."

"Oh. Huh. What, um—"

"I was a little rude to you earlier today," she said, folding her hands together.

Clint shrugged, aiming to be casual. But he didn't feel it. He was wound like a top. He hadn't had a girl this close to him in months, and his eyes kept wandering the collar of her sweater, then down further.

"Ah, nothing to worry about." he said, turning to look for a clean mug.

"I just think I might have led you on a bit and I'm sorry. I'm just—"

"In a *relationship*," Clint replied, enunciating with a pop of the lip. He gave her his most assuring grin. "I get it."

"Been in a long-term relationship before, have you?"

"Nothing to write home about," he said, just as the kettle began to steam. Steam was enough, and a good distraction. "But I've been with someone before who I thought would be," he said.

"True love, then."

"Eh, I don't believe in that. But a good match, the two of us. I would have stuck around if she'd been into that. But she wasn't." Nancy had gotten knocked up and wanted to be rid of it. Clint hadn't agreed. And that had been the end of that.

"Well, it's different with me," said Emily, scooping a heap of Sanka out of the orange-lidded can and swirling it into her cup. "I don't really want to get into it, honestly. I just want to apologize for being terse."

"He have a name?"

"If I tell you his name you'll go looking for him," she said, trying to conceal her smile behind the coffee mug. "I can tell you're that sort. You're jealous already and you haven't even met him."

"He'd kick my ass, huh?"

"He'd wipe the floor with you." She wasn't smiling any longer. "I'm serious, Clint. I don't want to do this whole jealous thing. So we need to stop hanging around at lunch and..."

"It's just cigarettes," Clint said, wishing he hadn't left his pack in the living room. If he went in to get them, it'd give her an excuse to leave. And he wanted at least one chance to get her in bed tonight.

"You know it's not. You asked me on a date."

"Tried to," he corrected.

"Just... let it go, okay?" she said. Her hands were shaking, and she looked away out the window.

"You spend a lot of time with your kids, especially with Walter. Maybe you should—"

"Stop. Now."

"Okay, okay. I'll let it go."

But Clint couldn't. He knew he couldn't, even as he said the words.

—

When November came, so did the rain. One day after class Clint caught a glimpse of Emily talking to a tall, dark-haired man by her car. She drove a maroon '69 Nova, and she always gassed it as the same place on Fridays. He'd learned a lot about her, even at a distance.

But this guy, the one she was talking to, Clint had never seen him before. They boyfriend, at last.

He was broad, all right, but not as built as she had him believe. No linebacker. Maybe he wasn't as tall, but he was fast. If it came down to it, Clint guessed he had the advantage.

The beefcake was older than he would have expected, too. He towered over Emily, and Clint didn't like the way he was looking at her. He was angry, and she was pressed back against the Nova.

While he knew he should keep his distance, Clint felt the familiar tinge of jealousy and a hint a most ancient possessiveness take over.

He had been polite; he had let her go about her business. But not now, not if she was being bullied. He couldn't very well stand for it.

The boyfriend put up a hand and pushed her shoulder back so she stumbled against the car.

Clint sprinted toward them, and he was shouting before he had formulated any cohesive plan.

The man's head snapped up, and Emily shrank back against the car. No emotion registered in her face when she saw Clint. Not anger or surprise; not annoyance or relief. Just nothing.

"What is this, your entourage?" the man asked. He had a subtle Boston accent, and his voice was deep.

"What the hell are you pushing her for?" Clint asked.

"None of your business," the man said. It was surprisingly polite, the way he said it, the words at war with his tone.

"I gather that," Clint said, looking at Emily who immediately dropped his gaze. "You think you're some tough guy, pushing around your girlfriend like that?"

"Clint," said Emily, forcefully. She put her hand on his shoulder and squeezed. It was the most she'd ever touched him, and he shuddered at the tide of lust it prompted in him.

Jesus, if she only knew. Maybe she knew, maybe that was part of it. Maybe she liked what she did to him.

Clint looked at her, and her eyes were dark like wet oak bark. He was going to say something more, but her stare was too intense. He felt the fury drain out of him and he frowned into chin.

"This is Bill; my ex-fiance," she said, gesturing her delicate fingers toward the man. "Bill, this is Clint. A colleague."

The men nodded to each other, and Clint grunted a garbled reply.

Emily rolled her eyes. "Neither of you should be here, so—if you don't mind—I'd like to get home."

Bill had his hands balled into fists. "We were having a conversation," he said, still all politeness in spite of his stance. He looked at Clint, narrowing his eyes. "If you'd excuse us?"

"You pushed her," Clint reminded him. "That's not just a conversation."

"Clint, I can take care of myself," Emily said. She had let go of her hand, but that feeling was now replaced with Clint's own thoughts of her naked, pressed against him. He swallowed. He was starting to hate her for it.

"Can you?" he asked, noting how feeble his own voice sounded.

"Yes," she said. She opened the door of her car and Bill shuffled back, wordless.

"Do you need—"

"I'm *fine*," Emily said, and shut the door with a clang. "Just leave me alone, for God's sake."

She pulled away, the tires crunching against the rainy gravel.

Bill looked at Clint. "Did you see a kid in there? I swear I saw a kid in there."

"I can't shake her," Clint said, the words escaping him before he could stop them.

Bill sighed. "Yeah. Just wait a while. She'll come around. At least that's what I keep hoping."

———

He waited until winter break. Christmas was the perfect time for casual visits, and so Clint bought a box of chocolates and purchased a little tree for her. He dressed in a wool suit, a thin silk tie, even put in a pin.

Apartment three. Around the back. He went around the corner from the street, clutching the chocolates and the miniature fir tree, his cold breath rising and dissipating about him. Lights were on. The snow crunched underfoot, the only sound in the icy quiet.

Her door had a little placard reading "Home Sweet Home" and a dried berry wreath.

He knocked.

When she answered, he had to hold his breath. She was done up, her makeup more pronounced around the eyes and her lips stained bright red. The shoulder-pads of her fuzzy red sweater gave her a slightly angular look, but the material showed her curves just right.

"Jesus, Clint."

"He's the reason for the season," Clint replied, holding out the chocolates. "Thought I'd bring by a quick present and be on—"

"Ugh, just get in already. It's cold."

She pulled him in by the cuff of his coat, and he staggered to avoid the ice.

"I just wanted to wish you a Merry Christmas."

Emily grabbed the candies and put them on the table. "You're persistent."

"Maybe," he replied, holding out the fir. He had expected her house to be cottage comfort. Instead, it was plain, Spartan. The table was unadorned, stained pine; there was a candle on the table, unlit. Basic white curtains over shades. Linoleum floor, no rug. It smelled like it had been recently sterilized.

Emily's nostrils flared, and for a second he thought she might laugh. But she didn't. "Well, it is Christmas."

"You really want me to go?"

She didn't reply.

"Is he here?" Clint asked. "The boyfriend, I mean."

"Do you have a cigarette?" she asked.

He wanted to argue, but it was too cute. "Of course," he said, feeling for the pack. He had opened a new one, just in case.

She pulled an empty green glass ashtray from her counter and placed it on the table. Clint lit the cigarette for her, and she inhaled softly, savoring it. "Been a while," she admitted.

"Can I take my coat off?" he asked. The house was heated with forced air, or a wood stove. Or both. He could feel wool prickling at his neck with moisture.

"Sure," she said, holding her hand out. He slipped it off and she hung it over the back of one of her chairs.

Emily smiled wide at him.

"What?" he asked.

"You just didn't give up."

He laughed, suddenly a little self-conscious. "I like you," he admitted. "You're..."

"I didn't think you'd stick around after meeting Bill. He usually scares people off."

She tapped her cigarette in the ashtray then left it there. When she turned to him, she was smiling.

"He is an interesting character," said Clint.

Emily stared at Clint a moment. "You know, he was just by. But he's gone by. He just never could stay away."

"Everything go okay?" asked Clint. "Did he bother you again?"

"He won't be bothering me again, no," Emily said. Then she smiled. "But I don't want to talk about Bill, if it's the same. I'm in a more committed relationship now, as you know."

"I'll have to respect that," said Clint,

though he didn't mean it. He couldn't figure her out, and until he did, he couldn't let her go

Emily laughed, a strange nasal chuckle. Then she took a step closer to Clint, tilting her head at him appraisingly. "Except you won't. I've kindly asked, in as many ways possible, but you've persisted."

Clint felt the unfamiliar flush of embarrassment. He had not considered that she knew the lengths to which he'd gone to find out about her. He'd thought he'd outsmarted her.

"It's both creepy and charming," she said, taking another swaying step.

By now Clint's blood was pounding in his ears, a swishing counterpoint to his breath. He was turned on. And he was scared. That was new. Somehow the fear made the closeness of her all the more powerful. She smelled sweet, fresh.

"Do you want it?" Emily asked. It was not delivered with the sweet sibilance of a practiced seductress, but the calm, matter-of-factness of a first grade teacher. "Now that you're here, do you still want it?"

He'd pined for her in ways he didn't even understand. She broke his cool. Emily Stevens was part-siren, part-virgin—this impossible mix that Clint was unable to detangle from his consciousness. He'd never obsessed about women before, he never needed to. There was always someone to move on to.

But not with Emily. Now she was staring at him, challenging him. Teasing him.

"Is your boyfriend home?" Clint asked. He caught something in the air, dusty and slightly acrid. He couldn't place it, but the sweet scent was gone.

There was a creak from the other room, the buzz of something electrical.

"Does it matter?" she asked.

Emily pressed up against him, sliding up his chest and into that kiss he'd been waiting for. He moaned against her mouth, warm and wanting. She was far from shy, gently slipping her tongue into his mouth and running her hands down the sides of his face, then up into his hair. He felt his skin tingle, then crawl, like someone was pulling gauze over him.

He shivered and pulled away, licking his lips.

They were numb.

Clint's legs were weak, and he staggered back, falling into the chair.

"I was hoping to get you to the bed, but the chair will do just fine," Emily said, stepping back.

"Sounds good to me..."

He felt his throat go thick, like he'd just downed some Novocain. His muscles were sluggish, moving toward rigidity. Had she stuck him with something? Clint's thoughts were muddy, but the overpowering sense of

26

lust was still there. He still wanted her, even more than before.

Watching with heavy lids, Clint saw Emily lean her head back and insert two fingers into her thick-lipped mouth. She pulled what looked like gum out, stretching it, and kept pulling. A long strand followed, slick and sticky.

And more, and more.

"You still want me now," she said, coughing slightly as she pulled the string from her mouth and then bit it with her teeth. "More than even before, don't you?"

He would have nodded, if he had remembered how.

Strand after strand of silvery web, she pulled from her throat and wrapped around him, tightening, always tightening, with her long-fingered hands. Sweat beaded on her brow, and she pulled down the collar of her sweater, smiling sweetly at him, almost self-consciously. She panted with the effort of securing him.

And he wanted it. He wanted more of it.

"Soon enough," Emily said, as if she could hear his thoughts.

"Is it ready? I'm hungry again."

The voice came from the door and Clint watched as Walter came into view. His cheeks were flushed, and when he smiled, Clint saw his teeth were streaked with blood.

"He's just slowing now," Emily said smoothly, running her hands over Clint's brow as his vision began to darken. "I'll let you know when it's your turn, love."

Then she turned to Clint and kissed him on the mouth. When she pulled away her smile was full of black webs and whispers.

Natania Barron is a writer with a penchant for the speculative; she is also an unrepentant geek. Her work has appeared in *Weird Tales*, *The Gatehouse Gazette*, *Thaumatrope*, *Bull Spec*, *Crossed Genres*, *Steampunk Tales*, *Faerie Magazine*, and *Dark Futures*, an anthology of dystopian science fiction. Her first novel, *Pilgrim of the Sky*, is set to release in August 2011.

Find Natania online at:

http://www.nataniabarron.com
http://www.aldersgatecycle.com
http://www.twitter.com/nataniabarron
http://www.facebook.com/nataniabarron

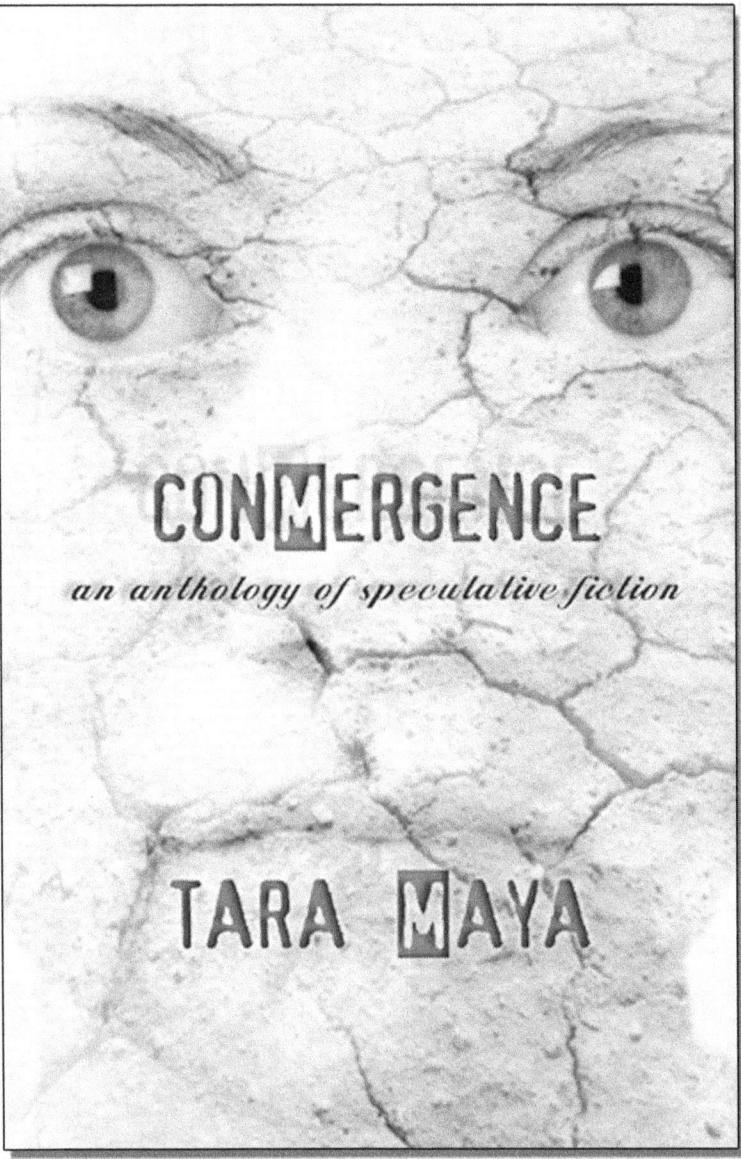

Conmergence

An Anthology of Speculative Fiction
ISBN: 978-0983107309

by Tara Maya

Fifteen tales of worlds colliding and souls falling apart...

Small Fish in the Deep Blue Sea

by

Frank Ard

Herein refugees from the sea, sky, and an idea called home...

"One doesn't discover new lands without consenting to lose sight of the shore for a very long time."
--Andre Gide

Harold figures I get a kick out of his emulated voices. The way he snaps shut the glassy membranes on his bug-out eyes and does a full-on boogie-woogie till his voice is new and he's a changed man. Whichever stereotypical recording he chooses hums through grates hugging the cartilage above his gills. He has a detachable emulator--very snazzy--so he can still use his true voice, but I haven't heard that pretty, waterlogged gurgle in months. Not since Sally broke our barroom pact and swooped on a Surfacer.

His affected cowboy drawl made me blush the first day I met him, and that's why he changes the way he talks now when he has something unpleasant to say. He's a showman, Harold. Always acting. Delivering bad news in a chocolate-sweet comedy coating. Laying it on thick so as not to upset me.

Clever guy.

Sally and I first met Harold at the oxygen bar where we worked, a lime-green plywood joint on the water's edge called The Topside. Fresh Surfacers often turn up at the bar just after they've washed up at Beachhead. That's because Surfacers have a hard time adjusting to topside air from the pure stuff down below, and we're the only oxygen bar within walking distance without a No Surfacers sign dangling on the door. The bar also gets a lot of snowbirds shirking their wives, owing to the fact that The Topside is a topless bar. A breath of fresh air, indeed.

It was deep into summer and the bay air steamrolled into the city, making everyone's vision hazy. The heat turned us Topsiders into thirsty, landlocked mer-creatures. I was breathless, swimming in my own sweat, yanking my collar when Harold showed up looking for a job. He wore black flannel and jeans, cowboy boots--spurs and all--and a red handkerchief below a ten-gallon hat, like he was an outlaw and the bar was a one-horse saloon in the badlands.

He'd found the getup in the second-hand bin the Red Cross set out for Surfacers, the place where Cape Town residents drop their Halloween costumes and other oddities they'll never wear again. A Department of Homeland Security work order shook in his hands. DHS gives every fresh Surfacer a form requiring local businesses to hire them, a free pass for the first entry-level Help Wanted sign, and we really needed a dishwasher.

Obviously, Harold hadn't emerged from the water too long ago. He was still lugging around the nylon backpack stuffed with newbie gear, courtesy of the United Way: terrycloth towel, sleeping mat, needle and thread, water canteen, kenetic flashlight, rain poncho, a week's worth of MREs, and an Army survival guide translated into the Surfacer language.

He had the same look as all fresh Surfacers. His mercury-colored eyes were the size of plums, each roaming on its own investigative track. He had a gumshoe demeanor, walking with an amateur P.I. swagger, as though he didn't want to touch the bar scene for fear of contaminating it. He extended his booted feet straight out, one in front of the other, so he touched land dead center of the tiles, as if walking a drunk man's line on a freshly mopped floor. Limbs new to gravity, he extended his arms like airplane wings to steady himself.

Sally was doing her usual routine, chicken dancing barefoot on customer's tables, flapping her bent arms, her little breasts bouncing, red vellum cape around her shoulders, reflective aviator goggles socketed over her eyes. Her dead and stuffed parrot, Daniel Boone, hung from her tartan skirt by a safety pin. Customers threw down extra dollars to watch her squish her petite feet into seafood platters, mash crab and cod between her toes, and kick untouched coleslaw and baked beans behind her as she pretended to scratch for seed.

"Fly away, Daniel Boone," Sally yelled, flinging the dead bird across the room, straight toward trembling Harold. The parrot whopped him in his slack-jawed face, and he fumbled like he'd received a long football pass, then recovered the parrot with his free hand before it touched the floor. As Harold walked the bird back to Sally, she adjusted her goggles, snapped the cape

"Don't know. But I'm gonna find me a new place, a real sweet spot out in the wide blue sea. That's what I do know. It's home, Stanley, like nowheres else in this here world."

taut to her backside, and launched from the table, yelling: "Fly! Fly away!"

But Harold was smooth. He dropped the parrot and scooted under her before anyone could blink. Sally swooned in his arms, then he sank to one knee.

"Thank you, my good man," Sally said. "These wings have given me problems all week."

"Boy-howdy, I'd better rustle me up some oxygen," Harold said. "It's gettin' mighty hard to breathe." He'd chosen Wild Jack Texan as his emulator voice. DHS gives an emulator to every fresh Surfacer, a two-way vocal translator, and most Surfacers donate theirs back once they can speak English without them. The voice sounded patched and far off, as if the original words had been recorded through dust clouds at a rodeo.

Sally whispered in his ear, then led him by the hand down the hallway to her dressing room. After a quick pit-stop to open a new can of clam chowder, I started for Sally's room to see if I could pry Harold from her clutches.

When I opened her door, she was lounging on her vanity, wrapped in a purple-feathered scarf, holding a box of oyster crackers. Harold squatted below her, fish lips open. Sally's legs straddled Harold's shoulders, wiggling her pink toes. As they giggled, Sally propped a cracker on her thumb as if preparing to do a coin toss, then thumped it into Harold's slap-slapping jaws. He masticated and swallowed in a gullet-grunting gulp, big fish eyes ogling Sally's skinny frame.

Sally, a red-faced tease, tossed her hair over her shoulder. When I removed Sally's feet from Harold's neck by her toes, she pouted.

"Whoa-howdy," Harold said, blending the two words into one.

"Partner, am I glad I found you," I said, mimicking his accent. His wandering eyes zeroed in on me. "I have the perfect place for you. Ever washed dishes?" I pulled him up and put my arm around his spongy neck.

He told me he was still refugeeing at Beachhead. That's when I asked him to move into the rental camper with me.

—

Harold and I are spending Independence Day fishing at Crocodile Rock when the sailboat carrying our dreams swims by. We sit on my pickup's tailgate, watching the waves slosh against its gold-lettered hull: *The Lady Bellipotent.*

Fireworks burst over the brackish water and sparkle against the diamond-shaped scales on Harold's face, crowns of rainbow tones glimmering down his back. He reclines, his slick elbows squeaking on the tailgate. "I'm a-thinkin' Sally has taken a real shining to me," he says, adjusting the glow-in-the-dark snorkel mask he found in the Red Cross bin. Made for humans, it doesn't fit right on his flat head.

His fish lips smack like flat tires. We smell fish frying, and we lift our noses higher, heaving breaths like Harold when he couldn't get enough air, back when he was still using oxygen tanks. He's foaming, thrumming his gullet. Drool drops onto his muscle shirt, forming a sort of saliva bib.

"Of course she's taking a linking to you. Everybody likes you at work. You're a fine dishwasher," I say.

"You ain't getting' it, partner. I mean she likes me."

The sailboat drifts closer, weaving between trash gondolas that waft toward the channel where the bay meets the open sea. The bay became Cape Town's refuse dump after the only landfill on the peninsula overflowed five years ago--roughly the same point when Surfacers began washing up at Beachhead. On one of the floating heaps, a seagull is trapped in a six-pack ringer, wings seizing behind its back.

"I want her," Harold says, looking out to sea.

"Yes. We need one," I say.

The canvas sails bubble and ripple. On the deck, a man ties mast ropes into pretzel knots, careful not to snag the deep-sea fishing gear. The man's family hangs out below deck, visible through large octagonal port windows. His wife fries their catch while their two boys laugh at cartoons playing on a travel-sized television set. The woman cuts onions, and I almost cry. When she cornmeal-batters the onion rings and drops them into the oil, my stomach growls. I want what that man has. I want to go on a sailboat, and I want fried fish and onion rings for my last meal.

Harold's cheeks inflate, and I imagine the possibilities. I think about how we would go far south, down to the tip of Argentina. Harold and I will knock around a Latin dance club where Argentinean women bounce in colorful bikinis and smooth men jive and spin in oxhide wingtips. We'll dance all night, then bring the rumpus back to the boat. I wonder if we'll ever sleep.

I say to Harold, "You ever been to Argentina?" I take a swig of Pacifico, then Harold breaks the news:

"Sally asked me to go to Buttress Point to see the barges."

I miss my mouth, sloshing lukewarm beer down my neck. It suctions my shirt to my chest. "We can build one," I say, pointing to the sailboat. "That life, my friend, is ours for the taking." I fan my shirttail from my gut.

"Well-sir, don't rightly know 'bout that. I says to Sally that we can mosey over to the Point, but she has to know I'm riding off into the sunset real soon.

35

Darlin', I says, I'm goin' home." He locks eyes with me. "I'm blowin' this here town."

"Sounds like a plan." I jostle a soda bottle with my bare foot. "We can build a smaller version with just enough room for the two of us, using this stuff. There's plenty of rubbish out here. We'll string plastic bottles together, to make the hull. Just us, you and me." I sweep my hand over the hundreds of bottles and scraps of cotton twine and broken wakeboards and flattened floats littering the shore.

"It's a whole lotta commitment, Stanley. Ya know?"

"Maybe so, but you've gotta admit we can build something that'll float out of this junk. Our very own design. A trashboat. That old tarpaulin over there will work as a sail." The tarp, once used for weatherproofing after the last hurricane, lay half buried in a sand dune. "What do you say?"

"Sally says we're all tryin' to find home."

The boat floats out of view, its image fresh in my mind.

Harold breaks the silence. "Where is Buttress Point, anywho?"

Couples go to Buttress Point to feel their way around each other's bodies while barges feel their way out to the ocean. The place has a long history of backseat sex, starting back when poodle-skirted girls and pomade-slick dudes bopped over there to ditch Mom and Pop. I imagine Harold and Sally in the backseat of her Ford Galaxie. Two people and a street-block-long jalopy like that parked at Buttress Point would make for a wild time.

"Buttress Point is nowhere you need to know about," I pull apart my fishing rod and pack it away. "I'm ready to go home." I toss Harold the keys. "I smell like booze. You drive, Lover Boy."

—

After we get home from work and I've packed Harold's sardine lunch for the next day, we lie in our beds, Harold on the foldout cot and me on the blow-up floor mattress. Twenty years old, the camper smells like the inside of an old man's suit jacket. The stench bothers Harold, so I sing a lullaby to help him sleep:

"I want to be way out in the deep blue sea--"

Harold rolls over and drops his speckled arm in front of my face. "Tell me why you left Florida, Stanley." His emulator voice mimics Cary Grant as Rhett Butler.

"Why do you want to know about Florida? I hate Florida."

"You got a momma back there missing your smiling face, doll?"

"Sure, something like that," I say. "It's been a few years, you know? Since

I've been home."

His eyelids flick, and flick again, in split-second stop motions, like in an animation flip-book. "Trouble on the farm?"

I exhale a small, shameful laugh. "You could say that. I got a lot of flack back there. Retirees didn't accept my lifestyle."

"That why you wanna be a sailboat captain?"

"I gotta get outta this shoebox." I try to touch his hand, but he moves it. "My parents lived in a suburban box where all the streets ended at squared angles, the houses like doll houses, Easter egg colors. Mom was a secretary, and Dad was a banker. Mom crocheted dolls, and Dad made me play baseball like the other boys. One time, I came home from practice with a black eye. They asked what happened, and I told them I kissed Ronnie Mills in the dugout. The first thing Mom said was, 'All the other mothers on the block will get to be grandmothers.' Dad strong-armed me into adjustment counseling. So I took off."

"Cast out like Eve in an orchard."

"What about you?" I ask. "Why'd you surface?"

Harold stays silent for a long time. I've almost fallen asleep by the time he speaks again.

"Don't know. But I'm gonna find me a new place, a real sweet spot out in the wide blue sea. That's what I do know. It's home, Stanley, like nowheres else in this here world."

I spring up. "That's a yes on the boat?"

"Sail away, O Captain, my Captain."

"We'll find our own sea garden," I say.

—

It's four a.m. when Sally and Harold crunch down the shell driveway, coming from their date at Buttress Point. I'm sitting on the plastic row seat in the camper's tiny living room, arranging magnetic letters on the cardboard Kenny Rogers cutout Harold and I stole from Kenny Rogers' Roasters after the chain closed shop in Cape Town. Kenny has a speech bubble over his guitar that once said something positive about fried chicken. We've covered the bubble in magnetic weather-stripping so we can write notes. Practical things: BUY MILK, NEED EGGS, or I HATE MY LIFE.

I've tossed and turned tonight with fervid dreams of Harold and Sally making love in the backseat of her Galaxie, their naked bodies sticking to the vinyl seats. To keep my mind occupied, I write a special message to Harold. We're missing the Os in our alphabet, so it reads: I LUV U.

Headlights streak across the oval

windows. I hear the car door thunk shut, then the creak of our porch milk crates when they sit on them. I lean against the door, bulging the aluminum at the bottom, and listen. Harold's detached his emulator. I haven't heard his true voice in so long that I barely recognize it.

"It was the skull barrels. They fell on our patch of ocean floor. Barrel rain, every day, landing in our hunting grounds, in the seaweed gardens where we speared the big fish," Harold gurgles.

"Radioactive barrels," Sally whispers.

"Papa and me were hunting sharks when I tripped on a barrel and sucked the sludge into my gills. I remember Papa's roar. He dropped his spear and swept me up in his arms, but it was too late."

"Too late. Too late."

I hate the way Sally repeats things like a parakeet.

"I started changing, began to float. Papa tied me up with sea vines and weighed me down with rocks. I remember Papa waist deep in seaweed, tossing vines to me as I finally floated up and away. The ocean floor dimmed, and he became smaller and smaller in my view."

"Oh, poor Harold," Sally says, followed by the sandpaper scratching of her fingernails on his scales.

Harold begins to sing in a quivering boyish voice: "I want to be."

Sally joins him. "Way out in."

"The deep blue sea."

"With you," they sing in harmony.

I change the message on Kenny's speech bubble. Then I go to our room, cradle my Bette Midler from Hocus Pocus plush doll. As I fall asleep, I think about what I wrote to Harold:

LUV U MAN.

—

Two hours later, I wake to the smell of eggs frying and the toady voice of Louis Armstrong along with his gurgling trumpet. I snatch open the orange shower curtain partitioning our room. Sally and Harold are jitterbugging to the music pouring from a wind-up weather radio, all elbows, scissoring arms, kicking heels, wagging fingers.

As the radio winds down, Harold notices me. Sally darts to the stove and flips a sizzling omelet. They stare at me and I stare at them, until Sally breaks the standoff.

"Would you like some breakfast, Stanley?"

I don't answer. Instead, I scoot to the mini-fridge, shooting Harold the narrow-eye. I peek inside our brown-bag lunches. Sally has replaced Harold's sardines with three hard-boiled eggs.

A new threshold of annoying.

"You must be hungry," Sally

mumbles, her mouth full.

Harold drops to his knees as Sally sits, then leans with his elbows between her thighs, his jaws open expectantly. Her mouth wide over his, their lips nearly locking, she drops the chewed-up bite into his mouth. He guzzles it down like a milkshake.

"He likes sardines," I say.

"He digests eggs easier." Sally wipes her chin. "Care for an omelet?"

The Kenny Rogers cutout stands awkwardly beside them. His message has been revised:

LUV U SALLY.

"I've lost my appetite," I say.

——

I feel detached in the oil rigs' glow. The lights streak the night in confetti colors. I work alone on the trashboat at our secluded building spot among Crocodile Rock's limestone crags, where stone meets sea in violent triangles jutting from the sand. Because of the stones, swimmers don't come to this side of the Rock--only lonely fishermen, grandfathers without grandsons to share the thrill of the catch.

I'm twining soda bottles together in convex lines, beginning the hull. Harold stands in the current in rolled-up chinos, seaweed-stuck and wobbly, holding his fishing pole like an overprotective lover. He watches the far-away columns of light coming from Beachhead, DHS flashlights sweeping the shoreline for fresh Surfacers. Shrimp boats drag their nets in the eerie black-green bay, bringing in loads of mullet and fat gray shrimp.

Harold hasn't helped with the boat today. Instead, he's spent the day reeling in fish and storing them in the cooler on my pickup parked at the rock line. I suspect it's because Sally is with us. Each time he brings fish to put on ice, he can talk to her while still looking busy. We've made a deal that she can crash our boat-building Saturdays so long as she stays on the pickup bed and doesn't touch the boat. She's been smacking on the sardines I packed for Harold, piling a molehill of cans in my truck bed.

The wind tumbles my bottles into a rock crevice. Reaching for them, I glance back at the truck. Sally stands on the tailgate in her tuxedo-print swimsuit, her rust-browned arms wide. Her cape glimmers purple and red from the rig lights blinking like minor planets. With those colors spotlighting her, she looks like a second-string superhero, her arms too small for her short body.

She tiptoes, then jumps from the tailgate. "To the moon!"

For a second, she seems to hover, flapping, snapping her cape, before thudding into the stones. She cracks her skull on one and lies limp, blood on her forehead.

Harold drops his fishing pole and sloshes her way while I navigate the rocks. He reaches her first.

"My wings ain't what they used to be," she says to Harold as he wipes blood from her eyelid.

Harold scoops her up, carries her to the pickup, and lays her delicately in the seat. "You're crazy as a canary toying with a cat. You know that?" he says, mimicking Humphrey Bogart, wet fingers nudging her chin. "Don't you worry, little one. Someday those wings will carry you away."

I run into the surf, pick up Harold's fishing pole and reel in. It whips hard, the rod severely arching, but the bite's gone, the fish bored of the game. Watching the lovebirds, I wish that I had never met Harold, and that Sally would tumble off a condominium balcony into the sea.

—

We share the bathroom every morning, the miniature linoleum floor our intimate piece of land, the tub water Harold's pretend ocean. He stretches out his arms like ship masts, and the eggshell wall tiles look like starched sails.

I'm grooming in front of the miniature sink in my silk banana boxers as he sinks down, his shoulders flounder-flat in the shallow tub. He sloshes up, and his eye membranes slide open. He looks surprised by his own wetness. His naked, muscular frame resembles that of a dragon.

"Yo, guy," he says.

His voice is not his own, and I know something is up: he's acting again. He has never called me guy before. It makes me feel anonymous, unspectacular, as though I'm just another man who's reached a dead-end in the minimum-wage maze. I have to go to work this afternoon. I want to pinch myself, wake up, and realize I've been trapped in someone else's life for forty-two years.

I suddenly feel naked, lines of myself in the double mirrors--one before and behind me--my bald head telescoping light from the bare overhead bulb down the three-dimensional mirror corridor. I poke my belly flab, pull my skin as if it were a rubber suit and let go. The skin slinks back.

Harold lists in the water, watching me with a bulbous left eye. It looks as though he is rising and my wrinkled, prickled self is receding, exponentially reflected into smaller and smaller images.

I plunk my toothbrush into my mouth. I have this thing about clean teeth.

"Yo, guy," he says again. "You in there, buddy-boy?"

"Yeah, I'm with you," I slur between brushstrokes.

"O-right. Tell you what we should do, big man..."

Old-school greaser. I've had a hard time placing his accent.

Harold bubbles his stomach and contracts his pelvis, preparing to disappear beneath the surface. He's been perfecting this disappearing act for months. Like an Olympic diver, he performs a nightly routine, training himself to stay under for longer periods of time, attempting to use his gills to glean oxygen from the water molecules.

Reverse engineering himself.

His gills tremble. "Tell ya what, let's you and me add a third seat in the boat."

I cut my gum with the toothbrush. The blood between my teeth tastes like pennies.

"What for?"

"Sally. Duh."

"Nope, won't work. Sally can't even swim. Birds don't swim."

"Ducks swim. And swans. You's forgettin' swans, guy."

"Sally's not a duck, Harold. She's too skinny. Ducks are plump. They have meat on their bones. And she sure as hell ain't a swan. More of a finch. Nothing special on the eyes and jumping with energy, which is nice, sure, till you wanna sleep or read or philosophize-- things that require peace and quiet. You ever wanna sleep again, Harold?"

"Well, I think she's a swan." Harold sucks a mouthful of air, slides under and curls like a seahorse. I'm halfway through shaving by the time he pops up, gagging. He drops back and strokes the faucet with his webbed toes, and I look into the hallway reflection of my pudgy frame. The half of my beard still on my face is gray, and my chest droops in a flattened balloon shape. I see only myself repeating on and on, a singular, lonely decimal.

"I think she's probably on something," I say.

He starts and stops, cocks his head, starts again, "Anyways, it don't matter whether she can swim. She's gonna be on the boat. Get me?"

"No, she isn't. We can't spare the room. Small as she is, she'll still add weight. Too much weight will slow us down."

"You in a hurry to get rid of me, Sweet Cheeks?"

I drag the razor down my face. I'm nervous and aggravated and trembling. I nick my chin. My blood dots into the sink like an abstract pointillist painting. "Also, you may not have noticed, but it's kind of our thing," I say. "Our escape...to our sea garden, remember?"

"We're blowing this Popsicle stand either way, my man. What difference does it make who rides shotgun?"

"It matters that it's you and me. You and me matter."

"Sally matters."

Feeling like a bully, I dab on mango moisturizer. The cream's menthol effervescence tingles, and I try to forget about Harold and Sally.

"She's my main squeeze," Harold says, patting his hand on the water. "You'll understand when you get your own swan, Stan."

"If she's such a swan, why doesn't she just fly away?"

Harold stares at me in silence. Water beads on his scales. "If you're a swan, you've got options," he says. He splashes down, kicks around a bit, sloshing water onto the whale-shaped rug. He winds his fingers with the grace of an angelfish, like he's zigzagging under the sea.

Only after I've gone to work does he surface.

—

The next morning, when I arrive at Crocodile Rock, soda bottles surround our trashboat in haphazard piles. The boat lies in two pieces, separated by a gulf of sand. Harold squats in the middle, looking smooth in a tropical button-up and flip-flops, sawing with a rusted multi-tool the twine I had so rigorously tied into Boy Scout knots. He blows fat soap bubbles from his snorkel, and Sally pecks them as they float by her face.

I plunge my hands into my drifter jacket. The sight of the boat in pieces makes me want to cry, or punch someone. Or both.

"Wazzup, Bro," Harold says as I trod up, kicking sand into his work area. "Gnarly day, eh?"

Dammit. He's emulating Hang Ten Ted.

I feel lightheaded, shaky. "What do you think you're doing?"

"Oh, this? Bro, I'm making the adjustments I talked with ya about. Remember?"

"Yeah, I remember. I remember that I said it wasn't happening."

"But it is happening. I'm doin' it now, big guy."

I knead my forehead with my palms.

Sally's sandals weight down a swatch of butcher paper on which Harold and I had drawn boat sketches. Harold has traced over our pencil lines with permanent marker, drafting the boat four feet longer with a third seat, repositioning the sail closer to the stern. Sally's sunflower seed hulls speckle the paper.

Harold's also drawn stick figures in the new boat design. The first figure has a fish head, ME scrawled in crooked letters above it. The second has a triangle dress, sinusoidal cape, and

SALLY written with a backward S. At the rudder, Harold has drawn an elementary-simple figure, labeled STANLEY in nervous script.

Most infuriating: Harold's new design looks like it'll work. In fact, due to the length and broader body, it appears more stable than our first draft.

"It's happening? Oh, it's happening, is it?" I snort, snatching the paper, waving it wildly. "Like hell it is!"

Sally squawks, hopping stones in vicious circles.

I tear the paper into fours, crumple and throw the pieces at Harold, causing him to drop the multi-tool.

"Whoa, whoa, whoa. Chill out, dude."

"Chill out?" I snort. "You bastard. You aren't changing our project, our lives for this...this floozy."

"Bro-man, that's totally uncool. Don't talk about my chickadee that way."

"Screw you, Harold."

He turns four shades of green. "Look-a-here, you're my main man. But I'm still adding a seat for my sweet bun. We're gonna be together, and you're gonna have to deal with that, bro." Pre-recorded waves behind his emulator's voice echo the real waves pounding behind him. "We got somethin' we want to tell you. Right, babycakes?" Harold grabs Sally mid-jump and drags his translucent lips across her cheek.

"Drop the damn teenager act, Harold, and tell me like a man."

Harold detaches his emulator. "Stanley," he gurgles, "Sally and I have decided to get married."

Sally love-pecks Harold's sandy gills. "You bet we have, Snookums!"

I lose it. I dive into the sand, steal the multi-tool, and run the outside of the boat, stabbing and slashing twine, snagging the blade on plastic. I pull the bottles free and sling them at Harold and Sally.

"Dude!" Harold yells, emulator back on. "Stop it."

I stab the bottles, pushing the blade in and pulling it out with exaltation, squeaking plastic. A mad rush of adrenalin, and it feels good. "Find your sweet spot now, lovebirds." I spit the words.

Harold tackles me, and we fall backward. My back crunches into stone, and we roll. His sticky fingers grip my arm, his scales rubbing my skin raw as he grapples for the multi-tool. We tumble on the stones, into the surf. Waves thrash my face as Harold straddles me and beats my arm against the sand until I drop the tool into the current and it's sucked into the bay. I shimmy my legs under Harold and thrust out. He lands in dry sand and scurries into Sally's waiting arms. She covers him in her cape, flashes her white-wide eyes and hisses.

"You," I gasp, dripping, trembling

43

cold. "You two want each other so bad. Fine. Just fine. Fly away together. Little birdie can take you on her wings-- if she ever gets off the ground. I'm done with both of you."

—

The pickup's squealing tires coalesce my thoughts, and I go home and sleep harder than I have my entire life, making up for my last few weeks of sleeplessness over Harold. When I wake, I pad into the living room. Kenny Rogers has a brightly colored message:

CAST UFF @ 5 PM

I scan the camper. Harold's things are missing. His poster of six-shooter John Wayne. His Sean-Connery-as-James Bond figurines. His gold-framed picture of James Dean with feathered hair. His pre-owned VHS collection. His autographed amateur boxing gloves.

The clock on the coffeemaker glares four p.m. I hightail it to Crocodile Rock.

The sun drops low, and a backwash of fog hangs low on the bay, soon to swallow Cape Town. In the changing light, I see the boat at the water's edge, as if it's wandered in on its own.

At the sight, I trip on my own feet. Curious whirls of sand kick up around the bottles whose red labels flap in the moist breeze, miniature flags. I blink, wipe sand from my face, and blink

again. Harold and Sally have completed the boat.

Inside the walled deck, they've constructed a sleeping overhang of broken surfboards, lashed with nylon rope. A PVC mast branches at forty-degrees, the blue tarpaulin bulking and shaking eagerly, a flying fish with multicolored wings spray-painted on it. Graffitied on the back is Lady Olivia. My mother's name. Just as Harold and I had planned.

I could kiss Harold, I love him so much.

The deck teems with Harold's Red Cross gear, along with hundreds of canned goods--enough to sustain a man for several weeks at sea. Scuba flippers line the inside deck, and on them alphabet magnets spell another message:

SAIL AWAY CAPT STAN

I gaze at the blanketed water. Harold's head bobs far out, his hand waving in long arches, nearly indistinguishable from the blue-gray water.

I shove off.

Harold swims some distance ahead, and I follow. The boat lifts on the waves, dips and rises, the design as impressive a thing as we planned. The sail spins, catches wind, then whips taut. I steer the rudder oar. I move with the boat and the boat moves with me.

The full moon looks like a giant amber-orange bubble ready to burst, so full with the sun's light. A harvest moon in an ocean of water-colored fog. I stretch my arms as I float under the bay bridge. I have never felt so new. I lean back to see the bright red arches.

I see Sally.

Fog spins on the bridge, as if holding her up. She's flatfooted outside the pedestrian guardrail, in tights and cape, aviator goggles rubber-banded to her face. Headlights blink and horns beep faintly. I start to cry. I can't help it, and I scream her name. She can't hear me. I watch because I can do nothing but watch. The current keeps Harold moving, his head craning to see her so high above.

She jumps. The wind carries her down. She falls, falls so far, the cape pinched between her fingers. Her arms reach like wings. Her tiny body plummets headfirst toward the water.

Then, she's up. She soars on a funnel of fast-moving air. The wind bubbles the cape, and she flutters her arms, a new bird in flight. She rises higher, nose up, mouth open, hair bristling like feathers.

Harold waves to me as Sally cruises over him. I wave back as he splashes on, headed for deeper water where the bay feeds into the ocean. Sally's shadow follows him. He watches her a long time, then drops under. She circles off toward the purple horizon. I coast behind, heading east, every exhilarating rise and melancholy fall moving us on our own currents, between water and wind.

Cape Town blurs into the mist, first gray-green dots, and, soon, nothing. Blue water surrounds me, and I am lost--lost, for the first time, in the restless motion of the sea.

Frank Ard studies creative writing at the University of South Alabama, where he also teaches English composition. In 2010, he attended Clarion West Writers Workshop in Seattle, Washington. "Small Fish in the Deep Blue Sea" is part of his master's thesis, a short story collection about animals. He prefers his animals anthropomorphic. Find Frank online at:

Website/blog: http://frankrayard.wordpress.com
Twitter: www.twitter.com/frankard

48

The Aetheric God

by

Kaolin Fire

Herein God might be heard, if not understood...

Asher hid in the library for five hours every night, from nothing more specific than the world, unless it was from himself. He buried that self in books, from the most ancient treatises on humours to the latest manuals on machining. Anything that quieted the voice of God within his head. His liturgist claimed rote would do, but Asher's experience was otherwise: repetition merely heightened the experience, the demands, the condemnations.

He knew better than to contradict his liturgist, of course. Asher learned well, both from his own mistakes, and from others'. Five warning lashes gave him the ability to imagine twenty, or two hundred seeing twenty on another man. And always, the voice of God calling for his own mutilation. But he was clever enough to see through the rhetoric, as well--it was not eye or hand that offended God, not truly. It was his mind--yet how could he cut out his mind and leave the rest of his vessel to do God's duty?

It was not his intent to learn. If he'd allowed himself the thought, a moment's curiosity at his proclivity, he might have taken the lashes instead. But his mind had outsmarted his will, and when he slept it chewed thoughtfully on every morsel he had fed it. It knew from research the memes instilled by culture and by history: it could separate those from meat. It could discern that the God, the God Asher heard, was nowhere to be found so compellingly as he heard it.

During the days, Asher attended to Father Isaiah--and had for the majority of his twenty years. He fetched meals and packages, dispatched messages, kept books. He made the odd prototype based on this or that idea Father Isaiah, as Chief Technician, wanted to see fleshed out. Asher filled his mind as much as he could with disparate menial tasks, meditatively letting any self-originating thought float away and fill in with some other random tedium. His mind, of course, was wise to this, and rarely let a thought reach consciousness--but it would slip the odd

The voice was gone. He waited for the recrimination: Cogs, One Inch, Nine Teeth. Cogs, One Inch, Twenty Teeth. There was only silence.

urge now and again, to further its purposes, a whim or desire.

Twenty-three beakers of aether collected at differing concentrations, elevations, and locales, and a recent treatise on steam engines gave his mind the idea. Asher didn't notice a thing as he laid his head down on the table, and awkwardly bored through his own skull with a small mechanical burr. His other hand captured the trepanned spirits with an empty beaker as they, by the laws of God and physics, began to disperse.

He was still in a hypnogogic state as his body walked to one of the prototypes he had built for Father Isaiah. It was a small mechanical man composed of quite intricate gears and springs, and the tiniest steam engine Asher had ever constructed. He opened its chest and expanded the accordion, filling it then with the aether which had until just recently been housed within his skull. He compressed the accordion, holding down the stop so as to store the energy, then closed its chest.

Asher came to, slowly, while counting out inventory. His head ached dully. The events replayed themselves as he itemized: Cogs, Two Inches, Twelve Teeth. Cogs, Two Inches, Twenty-four Teeth. The voice was gone. He waited for the recrimination: Cogs, One Inch, Nine Teeth. Cogs, One Inch, Twenty Teeth. There was only silence.

Was he so weak that the demon of his mind had truly cast out God? Asher bit his tongue, stamping the ground to not cry out. He feared for his soul: he had to confess, be granted absolution. Perhaps the lash would open his flesh and let God back in. Perhaps it was a test. He feared he would lose his mind, then hoped he might, if that would cleanse him. He ran from the room, oblivious to anything but the pounding in his veins.

Outside the now-claustrophobic room, he worried he would draw the wrong attention, and tried to slow down. Head bowed, he walked briskly towards his cell. He wished he were an anchorite, separate from the world and at one with the voice. If he hadn't fought it, if he'd accepted it, if he'd followed its dictates--but no, he thought he was smarter than that, he thought he knew what it wanted, and now it was gone. Now he was damned for sure.

He slipped through the Transept, picking up a relic cat-o-nine that had once belonged to Saint Ignatius. He prayed that the Saint would see fit to help him find absolution. When he reached his cell, he stripped his vestments and knelt on the cold cobblestone floor. Asher picked the cat-o-nine up, and, gritting his teeth, began to flagellate himself across the back, rhythmically, praying for his soul.

The pain layered on pain, slowly building up echoes of itself; he could feel his body, swinging, could smell the sweat and blood, the dankness of his cell; but at the same time he was floating above it all, separate from it. He could feel the same trance he had entered before, that he had tricked himself into--or been tricked into. Which was it? What did God want of him?

No, his was not to wonder. He simply had to listen: open his soul, and listen.

He imagined he could feel the ground shake just out of step with his heartbeat. He could almost hear the voice of God, feel it in his bones, like it was coming for him. Asher relaxed into the ecstasy of divine revelation, prayed to be worthy, prayed to be cleansed. He felt the hand of God kiss his cheek--and was flying.

He hit the wall with a gristly crack from his shoulder. He tried to push himself up, but his right arm wouldn't responding properly.

The voice of God was back: screaming death, destruction, obedience. It wanted his eyes, his limbs.

Twisting to the voice, Asher beheld: an angel of fire, like his steamwork man had been but a maquette. It had built itself larger, a frame that shook through the very foundation of the cathedral with its movements. Had it been an angel trapped in his head, then? Metatron itself, perhaps? Fire raged in its eyes, heat made the air shimmer;

52

steam flowed as pistons pumped, gears whirred, relay sparks flew. Its metal glowed.

Asher rose to his knees and prostrated himself before it, praying as best he could with one arm. It kicked him; he felt his ribs shatter like brittle metal, felt that he was drowning and burning. This was his epiphany. This was his moment. This was what God demanded.

This was everything he had been afraid of, everything he had been running from. But now he would accept it, accept the screaming condemnations of God, accept his sins and his due.

But this was not right.

This could not be the God he worshiped; he was insignificant before the almighty, yes, but this was not--

Fire belched from the belly of the beast, melting the flesh on Asher's side as he flinched. He coughed on blood and smoke. This was the demon he was born with. That was his command. He should never have let it escape. Asher cursed the irony...but it wasn't too late. He could hear it in his head, and it could hear him as well.

Asher stood and grasped the boiler door; his flesh and muscle fused with it in a flash, but he pulled, the pain fueling his fervor and desperation. The demon lived inside that boiler door, a plasma, nothing more than aether compressed and heated. He could take that in himself, once more.

He stuck his head into the beast; inhaled deeply.

Ringing through the rushing air and his crackling flesh was metal falling on the stone like bells, a heavenly chorus guiding him home.

Kaolin Fire is a conglomeration of ideas, side projects, and experiments. Outside of his primary occupation, he also develops computer games, edits *Greatest Uncommon Denominator Magazine*, and very occasionally teaches computer science. He has had short fiction published in *Strange Horizons*, *Crossed Genres*, *Escape Velocity*, and *M-Brane SF*, among others.
Find him online at:
site: http://www.erif.org/
twitter: kaolinfire

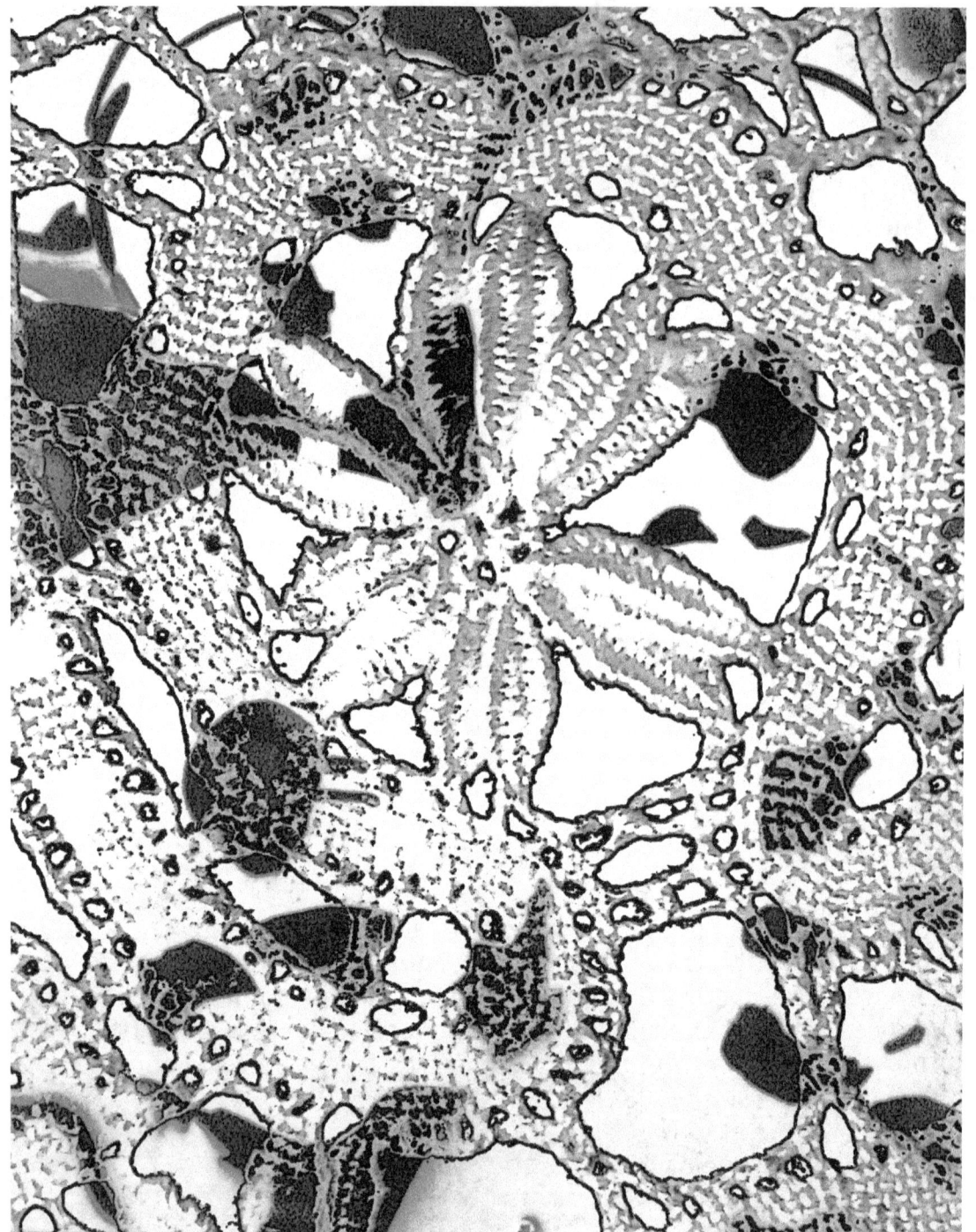

54

A Blessing from the Blind Boy

by

Alan Frackelton

Herein the mercy of God might be found. Or might not.

I

One moonless June night in the year 19__, a man named Juan Hernandez stole into the house of his former employer, the wealthy and ruthless landowner Páez, and left with his pockets stuffed with pesos and jewelery belonging to Páez's late wife. Still angry at losing his job that same day, and ashamed because rather than break the news to his wife he had squandered the last of his wages on drink, Juan had grown bitter towards Páez, with his land and his fortune and his house as grand as a palace, and in his drunkenness his mind became clouded with thoughts of revenge. That morning, when he was summoned to the Foreman's office only to be told that he no longer had a job, Juan had overheard one of the gauchos mention that Páez planned to stay overnight in the city; and so, as he neared the property sometime between one and one thirty in the morning, thoughts of revenge blossomedintothoughtsofrobbery.

And he was reckless, crossing the wide lawn to reach the house, then marching across the veranda in his boots; yet no one called out to him, and no lights bloomed behind any of the windows. Drunk as he was, Juan believed himself blessed; the first door he tried was unlocked, and the first drawer he rifled yielded nearly thirty pesos in loose coins and bills.

But Páez had a fortune, didn't he? Everyone knew that. So Juan, too far gone to remember that actions have consequences, pocketed the money and made his way upstairs. He headed straight for the large, ornate doors at the end of the first floor landing, opened those doors, and slipped inside. There in Páez's grand and spacious private suite, Juan quickly uncovered the jewelery, rings and pearls and a slender silver crucifix on a slender silver chain, in a carved teak box kept in a bureau beside the bed. Juan took the jewelery, and left the box, open and empty, like an insult, on the floor.

No one saw him, no one heard him. He was a ghost (he told himself), he was looked upon and found worthy by God.

II

Returning home late the next morning Páez was told of the robbery, and within an hour had sent fifteen well armed men to track down the thief. Their orders were simple: find him, kill him in any manner that pleased them, and return the stolen jewelery. If the thief had not already spent the money, they were welcome to divide it among themselves.

By this time Juan was wide awake and sober, crouched in a hollow left by a fallen tree in the hills above his village. He was desperately trying to convince himself that last night had been a dream, but the weight of the lie was there in his pockets, undeniable. His first thought was to run; his second, of his family. Juan pictured his wife Cristina and his young son Ramón, and his fear was real, but as he made his way home a voice as cold and alluring as the Devil's began to whisper *run, now, while you still can*. The whisper became insistent once he entered his house and found it empty; *they've gone to search for you*, it said, *this is your chance*.

Juan knew, then, that he would run, before his wife and son returned. He emptied his pockets, separating the money from the jewellery. The money he kept, the pearls and the silver and the gold he wrapped in a scrap of cloth, hiding the bundle in Cristina's sewing box. She would find it (the whisper assured him of this) and choose to sell it or return it to Páez herself. Either way all would be well, the whisper told him, *now go. Run!*

And so Juan Hernandez ran.

Páez's men had already picked up rumours of a drunk sacked from his job in the fields the previous day, and had beaten a name out of one of the workers. Luck was with them; before they could check Juan's house, a boy on his way to fish at the river told them he had spotted a man fleeing towards the hills east of the village. They caught up with Juan less than an hour later, terrified and too exhausted to fight. They took the money, and tortured him before cutting his throat (in one fanciful version of the story Páez himself appeared in the form of a serpent, and killed Juan by first consuming his heart, then his soul). But Juan, believing he could do this one last good thing for his family, never revealed where the jewellery was hidden. Páez's men knew they could not return without it; they rode back to the village, arriving soon after Juan's wife and son had returned from their fruitless search.

It all happened so quickly. Ramón was sleeping, worn out by the search for his Papa, but was soon woken by his mother's screams. The gunshot that ended her life still rang like thunder in his ears as he scrambled from his bed and burst into the room. He saw grinning shadows, and something faceless that wore his mother's dress, before a final explosion ripped the world away from him in a flash of blinding light. Páez's men tore the house apart, and soon enough found the jewellery where Juan had hidden it.

Pleased with their day's work, they left the bodies of Juan's wife and son where they lay.

III

Páez only learnt of Ramón's fate a month later, but the villages surrounding his estate had been buzzing with the news for weeks. The morning following his parents' deaths, Ramón had been found wandering near the river, blood still leaking from the bullet wound above his right eye. Clearly in shock, he whispered about lightening in a voice witnesses say was terrifying in its beauty. He was quickly taken to his grandmother in the next village, and despite the tragedy, the news seemed to be good; the bullet, thanks either to luck or the gunman's ineptitude, instead of killing the boy, had left him blind. When Páez heard this, instead of ordering Ramón to be killed, he sent for the man who had fired the bullet, and shot him instead.

Physically, Ramón appeared to adapt to his sightlessness quickly. Still, his grandmother feared for him. Ramón slept little, and poorly, complaining of 'dreams'. Lightning appeared under clear skies, even under his grandmother's roof, and this lightning spoke to Ramón in his dead mother's voice. Often he was unable to make sense of her words, but sometimes she spoke of *others*, and asked Ramón to let his grandmother know that she had found peace. If Juan ever appeared to Ramón in his dreams, the boy did not mention it.

He was not frightened by the dreams, but they made his eyes ache, and brought headaches none of his grandmother's remedies could ease. She had faith, but she was not superstitious, and more than anything she feared that her grandson was slowly losing his mind.

IV

When strange reports of a blind boy who could speak to the dead eventually reached Páez, he had forgotten the thief Juan and his family, and had to be reminded of the hand he had played in their fates. Publicly, Páez shrugged off the tales as nothing more than village gossip. Privately, they came to haunt him, the way dreams of power and wealth had once haunted him, the way his wife's death in childbirth had haunted him these past seven years. The jewellery Juan had stolen had belonged to Páez's wife, and was precious to Páez for that reason alone. Her ghost had been with him since the night of her death, but it was a ghost he could not see or hear or speak to, and so he held her jewellery instead, or laid her wedding gown across his bed, as if his memory of the woman who had worn it could animate it for one final dance. No one knew of this; Páez never spoke his wife's name, and as far as anyone was concerned she no longer even entered his thoughts.

A week after first hearing Ramón's story, Páez sent a man to the village to watch and listen and return with information Páez could rely on. The spy returned after two days, with the news that he had not only seen and spoken to the boy, but actually recognised him; he had been part of the posse sent after Juan, there when Cristina was murdered and her son shot and left for dead. As to the boy's powers, everyone the spy had spoken to confirmed the story, as many exhibiting belief as scepticism. The spy had spoken to Ramón himself at Cristina's gravesite, and heedless of any risk the boy had admitted that yes, he often saw and spoke to his dead mother in his dreams.

Páez found no sleep that night, nor the next. On the third day after the spy's return, Páez was seen, just after dawn, riding east in the direction of Ramón's village. Once there he was given direction to Ramón's home, spending no more than fifteen minutes inside (though he was seen to step outside at one point, taking a few moments to puff contentedly on a cigarillo). When he left the village the blind boy rode with him, and many of those who stood by to watch their departure swore that it was the first time any of them had ever seen Páez smile.

V

Ramón's grandmother refused to speak of the events of that day, but years later Ramón himself would tell the story to the daughter of a French general killed, along with her fiancé, in the Great War.

That afternoon in 19__, Páez entered the house unannounced to find Ramón and his grandmother composing a letter to relatives in S__ R_____. All that Ramón knew of their visitor was that he

Ramón, guided by instinct, allowed his hands to drift through the warm air above the dress, his fingers splayed, millimetres shy of touching it, and he thought *I am a child, I am an orphan, I am blind*, as if these concepts were new to him, vast and deep and impenetrable.

had once employed his father, as he employed a great many men from the nearby villages, but before the ink on the letter had dried he would learn that Páez was also the man responsible for the death of his parents. His grandmother, despite her fear of Páez (and who in that region did not fear him?) knew this already, and it aged her to keep her hatred for Páez out of her voice and away from her eyes.

If Páez picked up on this, he made no comment. He was civil, but spoke with authority, directing his words to the old woman yet glancing constantly at Ramón, who could feel the man's eyes fix on him, like hunger. And he lied superbly, explaining that Ramón's tragic story had touched his heart, even adding the spice of truth by saying that he, Páez, had lain awake night after night, dwelling on it. He had come today to make them an offer: he would take the boy into his home, feed him and clothe him, provide him with an education and one day a job. His status as Páez's 'adopted' son would ensure wealth, and respect. All Páez expected in return was for Ramón to honour Páez's good name.

It was at this point that Páez stepped outside, allowing Ramón and his grandmother a few moments to discuss it. The instant they were alone, the old woman leant forward and whispered into Ramón's ear: "This man is the Devil Páez. He murdered your mother and father. Go with him, child. Become his son. When you are old enough, or when you are strong enough, take your revenge on him, which will be my revenge also."

Before Ramón could respond, his grandmother called to Páez, and told him that they accepted his offer. Páez betrayed no emotion, simply asking Ramón to gather together whatever possessions he wished to take with him. As soon as Ramón left the room Páez tossed a bag of gold coins onto the table. The smack of wealth onto wood was final: the old woman was never to see or speak to her grandson again.

VI

Those first months in Páez's house were difficult and confusing. It took Ramón weeks to learn the layout of the many rooms, which to him all felt as vast as cathedrals, and to get used to the staircase which curved up beyond the height of the trees he used to climb when he still had his sight. On his first morning there, Páez introduced him to Louis, Páez's own majordomo, who would answer any questions Ramón had, and act as his guide. But Ramón was wary of calling on him. His grandmother's revelation was a stone in his heart, his hatred for Páez new and fragile; relying on Páez's servant for anything felt like a betrayal of his family. So Ramón constantly bumped into furniture, or tripped on the edges of rugs, and more than once he lost his balance on the staircase. Yet Louis was there to help him up after every stumble and fall, as if he had been watching Ramón all the time, so silent even Ramón's already keen hearing failed to detect him. But more than anything Ramón quickly realised that Louis was a good man, and loyal, and he treated Ramón without pity.

Meanwhile Ramón assumed that Páez's interest in him was connected to the murder of his parents, yet if that was the case, why didn't Páez simply have him killed? Now that Ramón was living under his roof, Páez as good as ignored him, and only made idle conversation when the met for dinner each evening. Ramón quickly came to recognise his benefactor's firm but languid footsteps and the stink of his cigarillos, and each time he approached Ramón expected something more than the simple 'good evening' or 'how are you today, Ramón?' Páez invariably greeted him with. Ramón felt powerless in his presence, and often he could find nothing to say in return beyond a hurried acknowledgement that he was well. Each night he asked himself, *how can I do it? How cane I kill this man?*

And he continued to dream. Not as frequently as before, but the dreams, and the headaches that followed them, like venom burning behind his eyes, had lost none of their potency. He spoke of the dreams to no one, and Páez, if he knew, never once alluded to them.

VII

Ramón had been at the house for two months. One night he returned from a walk in the gardens to find Páez waiting for him in his room. Ramón felt his presence, although for long moments Páez did not speak. The sound of his breathing told Ramón he was standing across the room from the bed, where Ramón knew there was a window.

When Páez did finally speak Ramón was immediately aware of a change in his voice, the strain of something Páez clearly found it difficult to contain. He said, "I was married once, did you know that? My wife ... she was an angel. We had been together for less than one year when she died."

That was all. Páez left the room, closing the door behind him as if to seal away the shameful fact of his admission. Thinking about what Páez had just told him, Ramón lay down on his bed without undressing. He understood now what it was Páez required of him, and he realised, with no pleasure but with an immediate lifting of the stone from his heart, what it was he must do.

VIII

Over the next week, which saw Ramón's thirteenth birthday, Páez began to spend more time with him, and gradually a clearer picture of his late wife emerged. Her name had been Eva, the daughter of a landowner who had once been Páez's enemy, until Páez offered a lucrative partnership that hinged on Eva's hand in marriage. The price was a considerable acreage of prime grazing land, together with the fifteen finest horses from Páez's stables, but Páez would willingly have paid ten times as much. Eva, he told Ramón, as they walked together in the garden, surrounded by the scent of jasmine and the chirping of cicadas ... Eva was exquisite, and despite the difference in their ages Páez confessed he often felt like a clumsy, tongue-tied child in her presence. She did not oppose the marriage, though privately Ramón wondered if this was more out of love for her father than for the man she was to wed. The year they spent together, with Eva's voice filling the house, and her touch everywhere, was the happiest of Páez's life. The prospect of a son - and Eva insisted that it would be a son - made it all the happier.

But the night of the birth ended in tragedy. Eva's labour lasted thirteen hours, and the son they were finally forced to cut out of her was tiny, ashen, and dead. Eva outlived him by three hours, before grief and blood loss overcame her. Páez, in another part of the house, knew as each hour passed that his happiness was slipping away from him, and spent much of that time simply staring at his hands, marvelling that he was powerless to stop it. When the doctor brought him the news Páez held up his hands and said, simply, "look at these." Then he told Louis to bury his wife and his child, and to this day had never once asked to see their graves.

Some of these details Ramón learnt from Louis, who spoke of that night as if Eva had been his daughter, or Páez his son. And it was to Louis that Ramón addressed a question that had been troubling him for days, unable to prevent it from corroding his resolve: "Did Páez's heart die that night?" Without pause Louis told him, "No. He has no heart. Eva died before she could work that magic."

IX

The first time, Páez brought him a photograph.

"She is smiling in this one," he told Ramón, handing him something heavy and square in shape, its weight explained by what Ramón imagined was an expensive gold frame. Trying to picture Eva's face he could only summon an image of his mother, then images, a flood of them that swept him away. He heard Páez cross the room and sit down, then the small explosion of a match as he lit a cigarillo. The ticking of the clock. Ramón moved his fingers across the photograph, but it told him nothing, and when over twenty minutes had passed without result Páez left the room, saying nothing as he lifted the photograph from Ramón's trembling hands.

X

The following night it was the jewellery which brought not Eva but Ramón's father Juan, indistinct but leaking a foul dark substance Ramón felt as grief, or shame, or some mixture of both; he could not speak, or lift his eyes, but his pain washed through Ramón, thick as tar. When Páez's voice finally reached him, Ramón realised he must have been speaking to him for some time, asking not "Is something wrong?" but "Is she here? Is it Eva?"

XI

Two nights later, Páez brought Eva's wedding dress.

Ramón knew before he touched it that something would happen. The air above the bed where the dress was laid - Páez crossed the empty sleeves over the flat bodice, so they framed the créme silk rose sewn onto the neckline - was agitated, fever-hot, and the room quickly filled with the scent of acacia. Tonight Páez stood by his side to watch, his breath sweet with the tequila he'd been drinking since early afternoon. Ramón, guided by instinct, allowed his hands to drift through the warm air above the dress, his fingers splayed, millimetres shy of touching it, and he thought *I am a child, I am an orphan, I am blind*, as if these concepts were new to him, vast and deep and impenetrable. His grandmother's words - he pictured her kneeling in prayer as she spoke them - were still a stone in his heart, but his heart was a song his mother used to sing, and her smile, and the love in her eyes as she gazed down at him.

Instantly the lightning came, filling the room by burning the air out of it, so in that moment Ramón could not breathe; and from out of the lightning came a woman as beautiful as Cristina, as naked as a lover. Behind her *others* shimmered, looking on with ravenous eyes.

"Ramón?" Páez's voice, compressed by need, was like a child's.

"Eva," Ramón said. She came to him. She reached out and framed his

63

face in her hands, and pressed her lips against his, and the kiss was her story but it was *his* story too. She was blinded by the bullet meant to kill her as he felt the surgeon's knife slice open his belly, she was scared and alone, the world screaming at them, and his life poured out onto silk sheets Páez had ordered all the way from Paris. When she broke the kiss Ramón could hear Páez weeping. He spoke her name, and gasped as if he could see her turn, watched as Ramón watched Eva open her arms to embrace her widow. But it was a different kiss she greeted him with, Páez twisted and bucked, his bowels loosened, and strand by strand his black hair dulled to grey. The kiss was endless, a lifetime, but Ramón looked on, his dead eyes leaking tears.

XII

It was Louis found them. Ramón, sitting on the floor beneath the window, heard the old servant enter the room, pause, and then move towards the bed without speaking. Time passed. Eventually Ramón asked, "Is he dead?"

"Not yet," Louis told him. He may have used a knife, or suffocated the moaning leaking thing that was Páez with a pillow; however he finished it, he did it noiselessly.

Ramón stood up. With his back to the window he could feel the sun, but he already knew that it was morning.

Louis sighed. "I know what he did to your family," he told Ramón. "But I have my duty. I can give you a day. At dawn tomorrow, I will come after you."

Ramón nodded. "Will you do something for me before I leave?"

"If I can."

"Take me to Eva's grave."

XIII

Louis had buried mother and child beneath a tree at the edge of Páez's garden, where Eva had liked to walk. As Louis watched, Ramón took something from his pocket, and kneeling carefully, placed the object on the ground above Eva's bones. Then he straightened and walked away, following the river east towards the hills and the world beyond them.

Louis thought long and hard before walking to the grave to see what it was Ramón had left there. He stared down at the single créme silk rose, and said a prayer, and then leaving it behind with Ramón's blessing he returned to the house. True to his word at dawn the next day he set out to search for Ramón.

As those who still like to tell this story are fond of saying, even a blind man could see that he did not look very hard.

64

Alan Frackelton's short fiction has appeared in *The Third Alternative,* *Murky Depths,* and *Title Goes Here,* amongst others, online at *The Future Fire, Colored Chalk,* and *Darker,* and in the Brimstone Press e-anthology *Black Box.* Forthcoming appearances include the new YA e-zine *Scape.*

Mission Statement:

Fantastique Unfettered, a Periodical of Liberated Literature exists to provide well-written, compellingly readable, original stories of fantasist fiction to readers. We will publish both established and new writers alike, and intend no certain genre as transcendant over another, though Science Fiction should be sent to our sister publication, M-Brane SF. Some stories might look like SF or Fantasy depending on one's perspective (stories that follow in the tradition of Philip K. Dick, for instance). We are interested in such tales. There are also specific areas of overlap that are outlined in our Writers Guidelines.

Fantastique Unfettered will continually seek ways to generate revenue with the end goal of paying creative talent the best rate possible.

Fatastique Unfettered is not a magazine. It takes many forms. Those forms include the near-anachronistic magazine. What forms will follow, we look forward to discovering.

Fantastique Unfettered is guided by a transcendant purpose and the concept that the Periodical, whatever its Form, is at heart an idea factory.

The Time Traveler
Leaves History Behind
by Bruce Boston

Listen, the vogue tyrants hiss as they drag a vein of dark stars across my weathered eyes. Listen, while desperado demagogues jostle for position in an already trashy sky. From the tangle of a broken parade they arise, wearing tin and leather, tossing batons and bloody confetti. Listen, they shout, like the clang of armor in my skull. Listen, they whisper, soft and warm as the talcumed thighs of a feverish whore. Listen, while ink pots burst open and spatter the clouds with curses. Flashy tumors sprout in the Sea of Tranquility. A veil of sulphur and serif gothic obscures the sun.

My eyes penetrate this stylish darkness, adjusting to disillumination. All about me the masses are marching and listening. Marching and crying for love. Crying like the whine of stripped gears.

Past newsprint and statues and plazas filled with polished public shadow. Through market stalls with gold flies swarming on their faces and hands.

Some have been side by side so long their flesh has melded.

They lurch forward in lurid combinations. Others chase adversaries up and down the shifting columns, hacking off fingers and toes. Even in the clock towers of the high city where the laws are set, where the hours are tasted and spooned from flask to flask, the ladies have complained of the noise.

In the metempsychosis of bone there is a land where ongoing catastrophes are assimilated and healed. In the transmigration of matter, in the limitless forking of time's possibilities to the Nth dimension of the dream solidified, there is a land where I stand stone steady, my powers revealed. A temporal sorcerer with no baggage packed. An artist from an eclipsed isle, my beard a stark presence on the blue sky of my shirt.

My tongue will be ribboned with light and my hands transformed to antlers of incantation. When the moons of my nails are full and brimming, I will climb the machicolated walls. I will tread the vaulted arches of time and imagination, tossing winged rabbits and incendiary doves to the crowds below.

Listen, I will tell them... listen one more time... before I vanish like wood smoke, like fire, like faith, like the fleeing tendrils of the soul's transubstantiation, into the boundless wilds of chronological creation.

Breaking the Spell

by

Rochita Loenen-Ruiz

Originally published in Philippine Speculative Fiction volume four, this fine story is Fantastique Unfettered's first reprint. Please enjoy.

You

There's this legend your father tells you. It's about a girl who sleeps in the center of a sphere. She floats in the air, tossed above the waves, destined to remain fast asleep until awakened by a kiss.

You laugh when your father tells this story. You've heard all the stories before. Most of these stories involve handsome princes on white chargers. You're not a prince, and you don't have a white charger. And you wonder what it is about a prince's kiss that's so magical.

You are determined not to kiss a prince. No matter that the stories talk about everlasting happiness that follows the kiss.

"Someday," your father says. "You will meet someone special. And when you do, you will want to kiss him."

Arcana

When she was a little girl, Arcana watched her father shape worlds. Shell worlds he called them, and he kept them under bell-shaped jars in the basement.

"Do people live on your worlds?" Arcana asked him once.

"Don't be silly," he'd said. "How do you think they'd survive?"

"So why keep them under the jars?" Arcana asked.

"Because, Arcana, strange things have happened before, and the jars are there for our own protection. When you are older, I'll explain more."

"Would the council send you to jail if something happened?"

Her father frowned and rubbed his forehead.

"I don't think so. But these worlds

are our responsibilities and it's not for us to question the council's decision to keep them under the bell jars until the right time."

One night, when her father had gone out to a council meeting, Arcana slipped down to the basement. She squinted her eyes as she stared down through the thick canopy of cloud cover inside the glass and tried to see if there were people like her on the world inside it.

She stared at the meticulously planted landscape, gazed in wonder at the green-blue of the rolling sea, and wandered with her gaze inland to where the mountains rose up to touch the navel of the bell-glass.

There was something there, Arcana swore she could see it. She saw movement in the foliage, and when she leaned in closer, she thought she could see someone standing on the rocky shore.

"Arcana."

Her mother's voice made her jump.

"I'm sorry," Arcana said. "I was just curious."

"Well, don't be too curious," her mother said. "You almost tipped the jar off its stand. I won't mention this to your father, but next time I catch you sneaking down here and peering into worlds without your father's permission, you'll get a good hiding."

Castle

In the spring, you go see this castle floating in the clouds. It hangs suspended above the ocean and from where you are you can see where bits of root and earth still cling to the underside of it.

A crowd has gathered on the beach and a lot of speculation is going around about the castle.

"Did you see that?" Someone asks. "It looks like there are people on there."

If you squint your eyes, you can see tiny forms moving back and forth. When they reach the end of the decapitated drawbridge, they fall into a stream of light that reels them back up again on the other end of the castle.

What must life be like on that castle? What must it be like to move perpetually from falling to drifting to rising up again and returning to the same old routine of life on a movable plane?

See

"You saw someone?" Arcana's father said. His brow creased and he frowned and rubbed his thumb and forefinger together. "Did this someone see you?"

Arcana shook her head.

"I don't think so, father. Would that have been bad?"

"I shall have to tell the council," her father said. He frowned again and stared at the world under the bell-jar.

"I wish you hadn't come down on your own, Arcana. You're not yet of age. These beings, they're not what you think they are."

"What are they? You never tell me anything, father. Why don't you tell me now?"

Fact or Fiction

"How did the princess get trapped inside the sphere?" You asked your father once.

"She disobeyed her father. She opened a box she wasn't supposed to open and these beings floated out and trapped her inside the sphere. There, she lies and there she is doomed to lie until someone frees her from her captivity."

You stare up at the castle, and you think of the princess lying inside her sphere. Is she dusky skinned or is she pale cheeked like you? Has she aged from waiting for so long for a prince to rescue her or is there some magic that keeps her fresh and youthful as the day she fell under whatever spell was released from the box?

"What if the prince is a wimp?" You ask your father. "Does it have to be a prince kissing the princess?"

"Maybe this princess isn't waiting for a prince," your father says. "Who knows. It's just a story.

Spell

In the night, Arcana heard music coming from the basement. It made her think of waves crashing against the shore of a world that looked like an uninhabited paradise. She tossed and turned, but no matter how she tried, she could not shut out the music.

"Maybe father will hear it," she thought.

The moon cast strips of light onto her pillow, and as she listened to the music, a great longing rose in her heart to see that shore again.

"What harm can it do?" she thought. "I'll creep down the stairs very quietly, and just take another look."

Her bare feet slid on the smooth planks of the floor, and she held her breath, as she caught hold of the door

Ugly creature that you are, what do you mean by stumbling all over my downs and scaring the hat from my head."

jamb. Quiet as a mouse, she crept down the stairs to the basement room where her father kept the newly formed world inside one of his bell jars.

Doubt

"Rumor says there's a princess sleeping in the castle," a man in a bright red cloak says. "They say whoever kisses her awake will win her hand and a million golden coins."

"I heard it's populated by ogres," another man says.

"Oh tush," says a burly woman in a yellow gown. "Everyone knows it's a trick. There are no princesses locked in castles, and since the death of Prince Jerome, everyone knows there's a shortage of princes in the kingdom."

The crowd murmurs and moves away. There is laughter and shaking of heads, and a general consensus regarding the cleverness involved in pulling such a publicity stunt.

"A castle in the air," someone says. "I bet there's a trick to it. I bet it's just another of those automatons."

Wish

Light emanated from the bell jar. There was someone standing on the shore.

"Who are you?" Arcana whispered. "What are you?"

Wise Woman

You've never been to visit the wise woman who lives in a hut close to the downs. But when you pass by her house, you decide to go in and ask her about the castle. Contrary to expectations, she doesn't look old and wrinkled, neither is she dressed in rags.

She wears a red apron, and has her hair neatly caught up in a blue and white bandanna and when you ask her about the castle, her eyes twinkle and she laughs.

"It's quite simple," she says. "There's a path leading up to the castle. If you want to go there, you simply have to find it."

"So, I can just climb the path and reach the castle," you say.

"There's a secret to it," the woman says. "But as with every secret, this one has its price."

"I don't own anything of much value," you say.

"I'm sure you've got something you can part with," the wise woman says. "After all, a secret isn't a worthy secret if it's not worth giving up a prized possession."

You touch your hair. It is long and

black and falls down your back like a rich waterfall of darkness. Your father loves your hair, and it is the one thing you are truly proud of.

"No one on this island has hair like yours," your father says.

Everyday, you brush your hair. One hundred strokes until it gleams in the sun and one hundred strokes until it reflects the moonlight.

"Well," says the wise woman. "What will it be?"

—

Snip.
When the first lock falls, you shed a tear.
Snip.
But you are thinking of finding that magical pathway.
Snip.
You are launching out on an adventure that will change your life forever.
Snip.
You will have done something no one else has done before.
Snip.
From here on, all consequences will be of your own choosing.

—

You hardly recognize yourself when she is done with cutting your hair. Without the fall of black to frame your face, your eyes seem much larger than they were. Looking into the mirror, you realize that you look a lot like your younger brother.

"Will you tell me the secret now?" you ask.

The wise woman smiles, in her hands, the strands of your hair dance as if they were alive. You feel a momentary pang, as you recognize what you have lost.

"If you go walking along the downs at sunset, you will see a funny little creature. In the native tongue, this creature is called duende, and if you ask him nicely, he might give you a vial filled with real princess tears."

"What do I need tears for?" you ask. "And why must I get them from a duende? Surely another girl's tears are just as good as a princess's tears."

"Do you wish to see the castle or not?" the wise woman asks.

You sigh. You've come this far, you can't go back now.

"All right," you say. "I'll go in search of the duende. What if he doesn't want to give me these tears?"

"You're a smart girl," says the wise woman. "You can do anything you put your mind to."

—

The Creature casts a spell

"Please let me go," the creature on the shore says. "If you let me go, I will grant you your heart's most secret wish."

"But you don't know what that is," Arcana says. "Besides, my father will be quite furious if he discovers that I've opened one of the bell jars without his permission."

"Little princess," the creature says. "Do you think your father will begrudge you a single moment of happiness?"

"I don't think so," Arcana said.

"Tell me your wish," the creature said.

"I really don't have one," Arcana said. "I'm quite happy as I am."

"Really?"

And when the creature said "really" in that tone of voice, Arcana couldn't help thinking about a dream she kept on having, night after night, since she had seen this new world her father had made.

As if of its own volition, her hand reached out and lifted the bell jar.

—

Out floated the world. It was beautiful to behold. Blues and greens and whites and violets, and browns and oranges, and there were myriads of tiny creatures spinning on the surface of it.

"Arcana!"

There was a crash as the bell jar slipped from her grasp and shattered to tiny pieces on the basement floor.

"What have you done?" her father cried.

"I. . . there was this creature . . .," Arcana turned to watch as the world floated above them. She was feeling quite sleepy and as she stared at the world, it seemed to expand until it filled all of her vision.

She could hear the worry in her father's voice and tears trickled down her cheeks as she thought of how he'd never trust her with his worlds again.

"I'm sorry," she whispered as the world blurred away and turned to black.

—

Duende

You walk along the downs, not knowing what to look for. A little creature, the wise woman said. There are so many little creatures here. Some of them hop away into the brush at the sound of your approach.

Some of them stand and stare before running off into the woods.

You remember hearing whispered tales about the duende, and you know the townspeople fear them, but you have never seen one and in the stories your father told you, there are no duende at all.

But when you hear the sound of whistling and you see the little brown creature gathering up bits and pieces of driftwood, you know this is the creature you have been looking for.

He wears a funny little hat, and he is thin and brown. His nose is pointed, and there are warts on his chin. When he sees you, he lets out a shriek, drops his bundle of driftwood, and at the same time, his hat falls from his head.

"I'm sorry, sir," you say. "I didn't mean to frighten you."

"Frighten me? Frighten me?" He splutters. "What do you mean frighten me? Ugly creature that you are, what do you mean by stumbling all over my downs and scaring the hat from my head."

"I came to ask you a favor," you say.

"A favor?" And you see a sly glint in the creature's eye.

"I need a vial of tears from a real princess."

"Hoo-hoo," the duende cries. And he jumps about on one foot and slaps his chest as he hoots out his laughter.

You wait until he has calmed down enough to speak.

"It's important," you say.

"How important?" the duende asks. "Are you willing to pay the price required for tears from a real princess?"

"It depends," you say.

"Depends? What do you mean depends? Either you're willing to pay the price or you just head on home to your mommy and your pappy and forget you ever saw me before."

"Okay," you say. "Okay, I'll pay the price."

—

"I will give you her tears in exchange for your song," the duende says.

"I will sing," you reply. "But first, you must swear on your hat that once I have sung you will give me the princess's tears."

"Damn!" says the duende.

And you realize that you were right to make him swear by his hat.

"I swear by the hat," he mutters. And he looks at you very darkly. "Now, sing." You think of the songs you learned from childhood. You think of the songs your mother sang to you. You think of festivals and of how the tinkle of coins and the press of the crowd held the promise of a future if you kept on singing. Now, as you open your mouth, you realize what it is the duende really wants of you.

But there is no going back.

Already, your voice rises in the air like a bird trilling to the sight of its sky. It trills and resonates in the quiet, warm and precious and pulsing with life, then the duende reaches up with his hat and the song dies away, and you know you will no longer sing as you used to.

"Beautiful," the duende says.

And he hands you the vial filled with the princess's tears.

—

The moon has not yet risen when you return to the wise woman's house. You carry the vial filled with the tears of a real princess and you hope it will be enough.

"Ah," says the wise woman. "So you really wish to climb the stairs to this castle, don't you?"

You nod your head.

"Well," she says. "We must head off before the moon has risen to its full height. There is still a lot of preparation to be done."

—

She hands you a gleaming cape and you see that it is woven out of what once was your hair.

"Wear this," she says. "It will keep you warm and it will keep you safe."

And she smiles as she sprinkles your head with the tears of a real princess.

"Now you are ready," she says.

And when you look up you see a staircase. It glows in the light of the full moon and winds up and around as far as

your eye can see before it disappears behind the castle.

"Well," says the wise woman. "Once you climb, there can be no turning back."

"Is there a princess?" You ask the wise woman.

"Could be," the wise woman says. "There are things you've got to find out on your own."

—

Up and up you go. Up and up and around, until you reach the end of the staircase. In front of you is a glowing sphere.

"Are you a prince?" a soft voice asks.

"I'm sorry," you say. "I'm not a prince at all."

"Ah," says the voice.

A woman stands up from behind the sphere. She wears a wizard's hat on her head and long lengths of diaphanous cloth dangle from the point of her hat.

"But the prophecy speaks of one who comes as a prince. There have been no strangers here. Not since Arcana's enchantment. Did you see any princes on your voyage?"

"Alas, Madam, I saw no princes."

"Well, I suppose we can wait another decade," the woman says. "I wish Arcana had listened to her father. I'm quite weary of playing guardian to a sleeping girl all day. And this isn't the most comfortable place to be exiled to. When she awakes I shall give her a good pinching."

"I'll guard her for a while," you say to the woman.

"You're sure you're not a prince," the woman says. She looks almost disappointed.

"I'm very sure," you reply.

"Then you'll have to go back to where you came from," she says. "No one may see Arcana except her guardian and the prince."

"But I have done all that was asked of me," you say. "I only want to see her."

"Well," she says. "This is highly irregular. I've never heard of anyone being allowed to see an enchanted princess unless that person is the prince of her dreams."

"I won't disturb her at all," you say.

"Well," she says. "If you give me your beautiful cape, I'll let you see her for a moment."

You take the cape from your shoulders, and you hold it close for one last time. Then, you hand it over to the guardian.

"Five minutes," she says.

She takes off her hat and hands it to you, and before you can ask her any questions, she's out of the door and out of earshot.

Arcana

"There's no help for it now," the council said. "We've got no choice but to let the enchantment work its course."

"But she's my only child," says Arcana's father.

"You should have been more careful," they say. "History is filled with enough warnings. We're sorry this happened, but we can't do more than make sure she's kept safe until the wish comes true.

In the meantime, we'll give her a floating castle. We'll surround it with spells. And she will have a guardian to make sure that only one who is worthy enters in and breaks the spell."

—

You

Under your feet, the floor sways gently, and you think of how this castle hangs suspended in the space between water and sky. You think of breezes rocking the castle, and you wonder what will happen when the spell is broken. Will the castle crash into the sea? Will the world vanish and become something else?

You turn the wizard hat over in your

hands, and walk towards where Arcana is.

Perhaps it's magic, but she doesn't look like you'd imagined her to be. You'd imagined a tiny little princess, but this princess called Arcana has strong, capable looking hands, and her hair flows like a lion's mane across her shoulders. Her skin is dusky and smooth, and her lips look firm and decisive.

You touch her cheek and wish she would open her eyes so you could look into them.

In fairytales, the prince kisses the princess and she awakes and the spell is broken.

You are not a prince, but if you try hard enough, you think you could make a reasonable enough impression of one. You stand there and wonder what it would be like to kiss a princess.

"And so the prince kissed the princess," your father's voice echoes inside your head.

"Fairytales," you say.

You shut your eyes, lean in close to taste her lips, and wish you were a prince.

Rochita Loenen-Ruiz is a Filipino writer living in The Netherlands. An incurable lover of the written word, she keeps an ever-growing collection of books in her small house not far from the River Rhine.
She graduated from the Clarion West Writer's Workshop and was the recipient of the Octavia Butler Scholarship in 2009.
Rochita has a website at:
http://rcloenenruiz.wordpress.com and maintains a journal at **http://rcloenen-ruiz.livejournal.com**

Holding Hands

by

Christopher Green

Herein a world with more questions than answers.

I was six the first time Emma Jean and I held hands. My parents knew her parents. It was easy being six, with her to hold my hand. I don't remember falling in love with her. It was too powerful a thing to. It made whatever came before it into smoke, meaningless and gray.

"Em," I'd say to her, "I've got a hole in me, and only ice cream'll fill it." Or soda pop. Or a burger from the diner down the corner that burnt down a couple of years later. I'd say any one of those things, whichever of them was on the opposite side of the street from us, and nearer. We had to hold hands to cross the street, you see. One of our hands would usually be sticky, or smudged with dirt, but that didn't matter.

When I was eight and she still languished at seven, she kissed me. Em was sixteen days younger than me. Those sixteen days gave me all the wisdom of the world, back then, back when all that mattered was getting big as fast as you can.

"Davie," she'd say, "tell me a why." Just like that, right out of the blue. "Tell me a why."

And I would. "Because the earth is spinning so fast," or "Because of all the dust in the air, my dad says." Whatever new fact I had that maybe she didn't. Sometimes my why would be answer enough to whatever question she had inside her, and sometimes it wouldn't, but every time, until the last one, she smiled and closed her eyes all dreamy-like, then nodded like it was pretty sage advice all the same.

That last time, though, Emma Jean cleaned me right out of whys. I scraped the bottom of the barrel, and nothing I had seemed to fit. We were thirteen, just learning how to kiss and really mean it. I was holding her hand, out there in that field. Everything around us was golden and dry, ready to be bundled and sold. Our hands were gritty with wheat powder. We itched from it. My becauses had gotten better, as I'd gotten older, but that last time they just weren't good enough.

"Because we came from the apes, unless you listen to the preacher." I was getting desperate, and Em knew it. She didn't answer. "Because we put a man on the moon."

Nothing.

I played my ace, the one my dad had taught me best. "Because of the damn Russians."

She didn't even blink.

"That's all I know, Emma. My head's

empty. Whatever why you're looking for, I just don't have it. Forgive me?" I puckered up and closed my eyes.

I'm certain that's how she remembered me, after that. A couple years later I got drafted, and the entire time all I was sure of was that when Emma Jean pictured me, it was as a dumb kid with his eyes squeezed shut tight, lips pressed together like he'd just eaten a lemon, begging for a kiss she didn't want to give.

I don't know what her face looked like when she said the words back in that wheat field. My eyes were still closed. "Why do my parents have to move? Why do they have to take me with them?"

I was thirteen when I learned that there are more questions than there are answers in the world.

—

So much of the middle of this thing doesn't matter. I drifted, without Em to hold my hand. I managed to get drafted just in time to leave a few pieces of me over there before it ended. Not enough to notice, just by looking at me, accept for the limp, but more than enough for my liking.

I started writing to Emma Jean on the day I arrived in Nam, and I kept it up.

"Davie, I got a hole in me that only you can fill." That's what I heard, at least. Out loud, she said "I've got a hole in me only smack can fill," or sex, or pain, or whatever else had made her into this.

My mail never got answered, and it never got returned. I almost gave her name and address as my next of kin, just so that if something happened to me she'd know, but I didn't. I walked through the end of that war with a hole I couldn't fill, and Charlie made a few more, with bullets or shrapnel and sticks smeared in shit. I plugged those holes anyway I could, but nothing took.

I swung, like a pendulum, between hoping the address was right and my letters were touching her soul, and praying that she'd moved again. Maybe someone I didn't know set my mail, unopened, in some drawer, unsure of how to tell a love struck soldier he was alone.

My wife, once all that was past and I'd stopped pushing the world away turned out to have Russian parents. Imagine that. Anyone who thinks that having Russian parents makes you Russian doesn't know how these things work. Kate was born in America, and it looks like that makes a world of difference.

Kate was a dancer, before I met her, the classy kind, a ballerina, not like those dead-eyed whores that stumble and strut through the streets of Nam. She teaches ballet, now, in a studio we bought when the last owner got tired of watching little girls not live up to their parents' expectations. On occasion, I take my walking stick and limp down there to watch my wife.

The main wall in the studio's foyer is just one big window, so the doting parents can watch the girls practice. I was the only one there, so early in the session, and I sat on the couch that'd followed me from house to house like a threadbare puppy. The studio had been soundproofed. Music that was all encompassing in there was reduced to the soft lilt of flutes and the thrum of a cello out here, with me. Just as well. It meant that when Emma Jean sat down beside me and I dropped my stick, nobody heard the clatter but me.

"Davie," she said, her voice a ragged whisper, "tell me a why."

Her hair was lank and her eyes were flat and dull as flint. I'd seen eyes like that too many times before. She was too thin, all angles and edges. Her skin was stretched so tight I was afraid it'd tear. She lay her hand in mine, and her knuckles shifted against one another like ball bearings when I gave it a squeeze.

"Emma."

Kate and her students had their backs to us. They watched themselves spin and kick in the mirror set into the opposite wall. Pirouette and kicked, I guess is the technical term. They held their hands high, and a few of them broke into giggles at something Kate had said.

"Davie, I got a hole in me that only you can fill." That's what I heard, at least. Out loud, she said "I've got a hole in me only smack can fill," or sex, or pain, or whatever else had made her into this. The whole room slanted toward her, ever so slightly, from every direction, like I was in a swimming pool and someone had pulled the plug. I could see the couch through her, right on through to the threadbare armrest. I could see enough to know she didn't just have a hole. Emma Jean was a hole herself.

"I missed you, Em. God how I missed you. Did you get my letters?"

She nodded, then shook her head. The hair that was tucked behind one of her ears fell across her face. "It's Jean, now. Just Jean."

"Not to me. Never to me. Did you

84

get them?"

"I did."

"Why didn't you write back?"

She shrugged. "I didn't know what to say. You always had the answers, and when you started asking questions, I got scared. If you didn't know, then who did? But you shouldn't have stopped, Davie. I got lost when those letters stopped coming."

All those small words somehow added up to a pain that split me down the middle. I saw Kate's eyes, reflected in the mirror. She flashed me a smile and clapped for the kids and waved them toward the bags and water bottles piled up in a corner.

I wasn't holding Em's hand anymore, and when Kay came into the foyer, she sat right where Emma had been sitting. Right there in that hole. The room still tilted toward her. Toward them both.

That night, I told Kate as much as I could.

When the darkness came, and the streetlights buzzed outside along a street I rarely had the strength to cross, Kate held me and spoke softly into the nape of her neck. I told her about ice creams on summer afternoons, about the smell of wheat in a young girl's hair, about the kisses that had turned into promises I didn't know how to keep. I tried to tell her a few of my becauses, by way of example, but they tasted like ash in my mouth, and I stopped. Simple answers didn't seem enough, anymore. When the tears backed off a bit, Kate asked me a why of her own. Why now?

I didn't answer, and she forced an odd little smile in the dark. I'd seen her give it to parents, when they asked how the lackluster kid was doing. It's the smile your mom wears when she tells you one brand of soda pop is just as good as another, when you know damn well it isn't so. Kate rolled over, but reached back and held my hand. I held hers' right back.

I slept, a little, and when I woke the noise that had dragged me from my slumber was not repeated. I lay on my back, my right hand holding on to Kate's, my left arm limp and asleep and hanging off the bed, knuckles touching the ground.

Cold, familiar fingers with knuckles like loose scrimshaw stretched up from under the bed and held my hand. Emma Jean whispered me a new list of whys, and I squeezed both their hands, determined to hold on as long as I can.

Christopher Green was born in the United States. After moving to Australia at the age of 20, he attended Clarion South in 2007 and has been published in *Dreaming Again, Beneath Ceaseless Skies*, and *The Tangled Bank: Love, Wonder and Evolution.* His work has won an Aurealis Award and been shortlisted for the Australian Shadows Award. When he isn't writing, he's thinking about writing, unless he's talking to his wife, at which point he is most certainly listening to what she has to say. Honest.

He maintains a blog at **christophergreen.wordpress.com** and tweets on **@christopherlies**.

Transcendent Purpose:

Fantastique Unfettered's Transcendent Purpose is to create fiction that is unfettered by tradition copyright. That is why our content carries a CC-BY-SA license. Our writers make their contribution to the wider culture by setting their stories free. Attribution is required, though we encourage venues that pay to do so in kind to the authors of these stories if one chooses to utilize their work. If yours is a small venue, then a loud and brash attribution is good. Sing your praises: that's often worth as much to authors as monetary rewards.

Five Oak Leaves

by

Elizabeth Creith

Herein, 20 minutes, some coffee, and payment for a tale told...

 Hey, mister!"

Alfred paused in the act of stepping off the curb, then continued across Queen Street. Halfway across, he heard light footsteps catching him up. A hand slipped around his elbow, and the little hooker – she barely came up to his shoulder – fell into step with him.

"I'll give you a blow job for those leaves in your hat."

"Don't jerk with me," he said. "I'm not in the mood." He lengthened his stride, but her shoes tippy-tapped faster and she kept up somehow.

"Please," she said, and her hand tightened. He took the curb and turned sharply away down Bathurst, jerking his arm. He heard her stumble, her sharp "Ow!" and the blare of a horn.

Shit! He didn't want her run over. He turned around, but she had already made it to the sidewalk, back on her feet. Her black fishnet hose had torn over one knee. Under the streetlight and the neon glare of the pizza place he saw a waif of a girl with long, fair hair, a skirt hardly worth the name, cheap strappy heels that should by rights be giving her a nosebleed. Her mascara would have done justice to a raccoon. She was way too young to be out on the street, offering blow jobs to middle-aged men. All around them cars zipped through the intersection and people walked or biked by; for all the attention they paid her, fifteen-year-old prostitutes narrowly missed death at Queen and Bathurst all the time.

"You okay, honey?" He peered down into her face. She nodded and wiped her eyes with the back of her hand, leaving two sideways smears. She took a breath and looked at his hat again, and the wilted little spray of oak leaves he'd impulsively picked that morning before he left Algonquin Park.

"I wasn't jerking with you, mister. I mean it – best blow job you ever had, too, or double your leaves back." She gave him a one-sided smile and he chuckled and picked the spray out of his hatband.

"I don't do sex with kids," he said, "but tell you what, I'll buy you a coffee and a donut at Tim's there, and give you the leaves, if you tell me about it. You look like you could use a sit-down. Deal?"

"You're not one of those rescuers?" she said, "Trying to get me off the street?"

On impulse he tore two leaves off their twig and held them out to her.

"Look, two now, the other three when you've told me the story, okay? They'll kick us out of Tim's in twenty minutes anyway, so - "

S he slid into the booth across from him.

"That's better," he said, and pushed her plate – two jelly donuts – encouragingly towards her. She'd washed her makeup off while he ordered; without it she looked younger, and also more serious. Her hazel eyes flashed green. She finished her first donut in thirty seconds and took a gulp of the hot chocolate she'd asked for.

"Ready to tell me?" he asked.

"Sure. You're not going to believe it, though."

 Well, you know, selling stories is a little bit like

"Well, you know, selling stories is a little bit like selling sex. It doesn't have to be real, it just has to be good enough to entertain them, fool them, just for the moment, right? Make it good enough, I'll believe it, just for now. Maybe even in the morning."

selling sex. It doesn't have to be real, it just has to be good enough to entertain them, fool them, just for the moment, right? Make it good enough, I'll believe it, just for now. Maybe even in the morning."

She chewed her lip, considering.

"All right," she said, "I'm a changeling. Do you know what that is?"

He shook his head.

"The elves leave one of their babies in place of a human one. I was left for a human. I'm going home to my real people, the elves." She paused.

"Go on."

"Changelings mostly didn't survive," she said, "The stories say they sickened and died. The ones that didn't, people used to find out what they were and kill them. But now, if your kid's sick, you take them to the doctor, maybe a specialist. I spent a lot of time sick in bed, but I didn't die. Then when I - " she glanced sideways.

An embarrassed hooker, he thought, who'd believe it? Aloud he said, "You hit puberty?"

"Yeah. I began to hear them - elves - calling me. In school, on the bus, everywhere. I didn't tell anybody. They'd lock me up. And then some things, metal and stuff, started to hurt me, just touching it. I hear plants, too. The little trees in those planters? They can't reach the earth, and they cry all the time. I have to leave."

"So where are you going?" he asked.

"I didn't know until tonight," she said. "I saw those leaves, and I knew they came from my home. Where did you get them?"

"Algonquin Park. I go camping up there a couple of times every year."

"Can I get a bus to there?"

"Close - there's a little place called Maynooth right nearby. You can get a shuttle to the park from there."

"To where you got those leaves. That's my home; I knew when I saw them."

"Algonquin Park. It's up north. I go camping there twice a year."

"Can I get a bus there?"

"Sure. But - what about your parents?"

She touched his wrist. "Where did you say you got these?"

He opened his mouth, and thought, Algonquin Park. But that couldn't be right. There was no such place.

She touched his wrist again.

"See?" she said, "Algonquin Park. It's real. My parents won't even remember me."

"How did you do that?"

She shrugged, all adolescent for a moment.

"I dunno. I just can. Look at this!" She took the two leaves from her little purse and laid them side by side on the table, then smoothed one with her hand. It crinkled and fluttered; in its place a fifty-dollar bill settled onto the white Formica, hologram shimmering.

Alfred picked it up, felt the engraving.

"If you can do that with leaves, why are you hooking?" he asked.

"The leaves here – they're poisoned or something. They'll turn, but then they crumble up and blow away. These will last until sunrise. I need to get my ticket tonight."

Alfred took the three remaining leaves out of his hat and passed them over to her.

"Do it again," he said, laying his arm along the side of the table to shield the leaves. She smiled and spread the leaves out, and again he watched that flutter-and-crinkle.

"I gotta go," she said. She folded the fifties into her purse and ate the remaining jelly donut in three bites.

"Is that enough money?" he asked.

"I've got some, cash, too."

"So no more blow jobs for strange men."

"No. No more. I – I can't say the usual words, you know? We can't. But I owe you."

"Not at all. You sold me a helluva story. Maybe I'll see you in Algonquin Park."

"Maybe." She smiled and stood, then leaned down and kissed his cheek. Through the window Alfred watched her walk away toward Bay and the bus station; the light at Queen and Bathurst turned as she reached it, and she never broke stride

Are there others like her? he wondered. In the dregs of his coffee he saw his future, cruising Queen Street with oak leaves in his hat, rescuing elfin hookers.

Elizabeth Creith draws on her familiarity with history, myth and folklore to write her fiction and poetry. For ten years she wrote humour and commentary for CBC radio. She has had stories published in *New Myths, Chicken Soup for the Soul, The Linnet's Wings* and *THEMA*, among others. Her flash "Dark Chocolate" took first place in the Northwestern Ontario Writers' Workshop 2010 writing contest.

Elizabeth lives, writes and commits art in Wharncliffe, Northern Ontario, distracted occasionally by her husband, dog and cat. She blogs about art and writing at **http://ecreith.wordpress.com**

Portrait of My Dead Brother with Burning Wing
after Dali
by Bruce Boston

An immature boy in a sailor suit
refuses to leave

the beaches of Port Ligat.
The great masturbator

considers the obscene history
of the Third Reich.

Somewhere in the analytic
reaches of space-time

a nightstand commanders
the consciousness of crutches,

a burning wing, bodiless,
infests the earth with its seed.

A still life of fish and fruit
rots on an oaken table.

The omphalos of illicit desire
taunts his dreams as if it were

an implacable crucifix
carved from blood and flesh.

The Driftwood Chair

by

Michael J. DeLuca

Herein paths falter amid gestures mimicked and waters black.

David walked north along Nauset beach at dawn. A chair made him stop, when night and cold and exhaustion had not: a chair, waterlogged, stained but not rotten, the wood smoothed and rounded by ages of drifting, its legs in the air. He heaved it out of the sand, leaving hollows behind that caved as he righted it. He rolled his trouser-cuffs higher, pushed back his shirt sleeves, and sat. He leaned over his knees, bare toes dug into the freezing cold beach at the very edge of the ocean.

A wave crashed past him, caught the sand as high as it could reach and pulled. Land slid out from under David's heels, and he sank another quarter-inch. Of the line of his footprints leading south, back towards his life, the closest section disappeared.

The morning mists obscured the shore, mirrored the waves, the voids of their billows and curves foiling linear thought by the constant illusion of motion. This vertigo the chair arrested, providing a frame of reference all its own.

Out of the mists, a pale girl appeared. She wore a black bathing suit, had straight brown hair and carried a towel.

She wasn't at all like Eleanora.

"Good morning," she said.

David acknowledged, his voice barely audible above the surf.

She dropped the towel at the edge of the dry part of the beach, ran towards the water kicking up sand as though it were foam, and dove into the face of a wave. The roaring solitude returned. She reappeared among gray swells, swimming.

The fog's veil drew back, revealing the sun. David hadn't slept; the bright hurt his eyes. Eleanora after she'd betrayed him, sitting on the open windowsill in white.

No, she had never worn white.

Another wave hit its peak and toppled; the girl emerged, surfacing out of the whitecap like a ship's figurehead. The wave rolled her onto the shore. David folded his fingers over his aching eyes.

"Are you staying with the Magdalas?"

"No."

"The Roches?"

"I walked here."

"Walked from where?"

"From the Chatham Light."

" That's twenty miles."

David waited, then parted his fingers. She was still there, drying her hair. He closed them again.

"It must be a beautiful walk," she said.

He remembered the night. The Milky Way above the dunes. The Nauset Light. The black hole in his stomach. The howls of birds.

He forced his legs straight and reached for his toes. His muscles ached as only twenty miles of sand can make them. He stretched until the pain shot up his calves and thighs and flashed red-black behind his eyes.

When he no longer felt the sun, he looked. The gray veil had closed. The waves had smoothed away his footprints. She was still there.

"I stopped for a rest," he said. "Then I'll go on."

"How far are you going?"

"To Race Point."

"The whole Outer Cape? Why?"

He gripped the chair.

The girl wrapped the towel around her waist and pulled back her damp, dark hair. "I hope you make it," she said, as though to deny all his efforts at incivility. She walked up the beach.

The sun rose and burned back the mist. There were voices in the sawgrass, then the creak of wood and figures on the stairs.

The sand sprouted fat people, screaming children, bamboo mats and umbrellas. The reek of sunblock overpowered the brine. Among the gray waves far out where no one swam, sailboats passed, one or two in an hour.

A hard-bodied lifeguard and a girl in a bikini strolled by, arms around each other's waists, blocking his view. A whisper. A giggle. The subtle motion of a hand. He despised them. He despised their stupid innocence, their mimicked gestures. Puppets. Puppets of love, a thing they could not understand.

On the north horizon, where he ought to be, mirages shimmered over baking sand. He ought to be walking. Shrill children with shovels and pails dug moats and built castles around him.

Eleanora's fingerprints on empty glasses. Her shoes by the door. Red-gold hair on her brush. Her bottles lined against the bathroom mirror, bookended by lumps of flesh. His skin began to burn. He dragged the chair under the wooden stairs and sat in the slatted shadows. The sun rolled towards the dunes.

The human chaos dismantled itself and lumbered up the stairs to the parking lots and changing rooms. A

Silly, stubborn Kate, their faces said. Still digging washed-up treasures from the sand. Still trying to fix them.

beachball had caught on the tip of a whitecap, forgotten, pushed east by the wind, pulled west by the current, constantly rolling, going nowhere.

David dozed; he woke to footsteps. The dunes cast shadows beneath a violet sky. He dragged the chair back into the sun, stepping over moats and castles already washing out to sea. The dark-haired girl met him emerging from her swim. "I figured you'd have gone," she said.

She was shorter than Eleanora. Eleanora's head had fit under his chin. And when he knelt.... "I can't decide. I might go back."

"But you're halfway already."

"You're right." He sank into the chair. "Maybe I'll sit here forever."

She walked around him, around the chair, leaving clean footprints in the wet sand. In each imprint, the middle toe was slightly too long. "It's a beautiful chair. Did you see what's carved here?"

He got up and turned the chair on one leg. On the back of the headrest was carved a shallow relief of a seal, the detail worn away. Dim words, illegible. "*Le Phoque Gris*," he guessed. "A ship?"

"I'd like to borrow it sometime. After you're done with it, I mean. To paint."

"What--restore it? I like it how it is."

"No, no--to paint a picture. A landscape maybe. It's interesting, don't you think? A driftwood chair."

Her eyes were green like Eleanora's.

102

He hated himself for looking.

The shadow of the dunes had reached the surf. Chill breezes raced the water, brushing his ankles and sunburned neck, sucking warmth away like leeches. "I better get home and get dry," she said.

He unrolled the sleeves of his shirt, buttoned the cuffs.

"Have you got someplace to sleep?"

He looked at the chair.

"Have you eaten?"

"At the hot dog stand." He hadn't.

She headed for the stairs. Her footprints lost their shape, became oval hollows among numberless others. Then she came back and held out a hand. Eleanora's, french-manicured, white-knuckled gripping the bedpost.

"I'm Kate."

"David," he said, flinching.

She folded her arms. "So why are you doing this, David?"

He unrolled a thumb from one of his fists and jerked it north. "That way, somewhere between here and Race Point, I get over her." He opened a finger from the same fist, pointing south. "The other way I forgive her."

Finally, he'd made her uncomfortable. He looked at his toes, curled them up gripping the sand.

"Guess I'll see you in the morning, then." Her hair cast cold salt across him as she turned.

He pulled the chair into the lee of a

dune, unrolled his pants, buttoned his shirt to his throat and sat hugging his knees. A tern screamed among the marshes. He leaned his head back against the chair and slept.

At dawn, she dropped her towel beside him without stopping, ran for the water and dove.

David waited for her at the water line, hands in his pockets, shifting from foot to foot. She emerged. "It gets cold at night," he said."

"You could have kept walking," she answered, dripping. She wrapped the towel around her. Part of it came off and slipped to the sand. He realized she'd brought two.

"What's that for?"

"I thought you might want it--to swim."

"It's freezing."

"Everyone says that. It's not so bad. The shock clears the head."

"Too cold," he said.

She shrugged. "So use it as a blanket."

He wrapped the towel around his shoulders. It was warm. He sat in the sand at the high water line, hugged his knees and closed the towel around them.

Kate's footsteps scrunched away, then scrunched back, something dragging behind. She settled the driftwood chair and sat, spreading her towel over her lap. She crossed her ankles.

"How'd you sleep?"

"That ship, the *Gray Seal*, le *Phoque Gris*. It's a sailing ship, a pleasure ship, from the Bay of Biscay. There was a party on deck, and she--she wanted to dance. I wouldn't. She danced with the captain instead. She'd come over between songs. Kiss me. Then she'd go back. I just sat in the chair."

Razor-clam holes bubbled as a wave pulled back from the sand. "A nightmare." The corners of her towel fluttered. "You think it's trying to tell you something?"

"What? The chair?"

A wrinkle appeared above her nose. "The dream."

He squeezed sleep-sand from his eyes. A gull splashed, diving for fish.

Footsteps on the stairs. The first of the day's beachgoers, an elderly couple hand in hand. They teetered past like toddlers, leaning on each other as the sand shifted.

"You know what?" he said, once they were out of earshot. "It was a nightmare, but I didn't want it to end. I just wanted her to kiss me."

She stood, wrapping the towel around her waist.

"Come on. You can't sit here. You'll go crazy. You'll get sunburned to death. I could use a drink--you want a soda?"

She led the way up the wooden stairs.

He studied the curve of her spine. There were freckles. Not like Eleanora's.

In the parking lot, he stopped. "Wait."

He went back and heaved the chair into the sawgrass, out of sight.

They had cranberry-lime rickeys, tart and red. David asked for more sugar.

They played mini-golf on a course she'd been to as a kid. One of the holes was a giant plaster whale. You had to putt down into the blowhole; the ball rolled out its mouth. She talked about the Cape in winter. They got ice cream and sat on a bench overlooking the dunes.

Clouds arrived from the ocean. The parking lots emptied. They walked back to her house. "It was my parents'." A faded yellow bungalow with white lattices, grapes growing out of control and an easel in the garden. "Want to see?"

Most of the canvas was blank. In the center left, surrounded by faint, sketched stormy ocean and rocky shore, a seal curled on a promontory, neck twisted towards the viewer, jaws open in a vicious bark. There was black in its mouth.

She closed the door to the house and handed him a drink. He gulped without comment. The seal's gullet yawned.

"So?"

After a whole day with her, bewildered, he'd spent two minutes in her garden, and he knew her. Spiral periwinkle shells and sand-smoothed stones lined the flowerbeds. Inside, tortured hulks of driftwood leaned against the windowpanes. On the door was a leaded mosaic of sea-glass, brown, blue and green: a cloud crossing the sun.

A beachcomber. A scavenger.

She was grieving.

"I don't know," he said. "It's...full of emotion."

She took it off the easel as if it didn't matter, shoved it under her arm. She gestured with her drink at the sky. "It's going to rain tonight. You better not sleep on the beach."

"Watch me," he said.

"Don't be stupid. You thought it was cold last night? You'll get pneumonia. If you kept moving maybe, kept walking. Not if you just sit in that chair."

"I can't keep walking."

"Why not?"

"What if I get to the end of the beach and it isn't long enough? I'd have to swim."

Her flip-flops clapped against the flagstone. She elbowed open the door. "What I'm trying to say, David, is if you want, I can let you sleep here."

The face of the painting hovered, oblique, half in shadow. In the white space behind the angry seal his mind put a ship tilting in a gale. Red hair whipped from the aft deck. He reached into imagined wind and snatched a ribbon.

She never wore ribbons.

His throat was unbearably dry. He finished what was in the glass.

"Not with *me*, asshole," said Kate. "You can sleep on the couch. I can lend you a pillow. You could take a shower."

"I'll be fine. I'll... buy a tarp in town and sleep under that." He set the glass hurriedly on a flagstone and walked down the driveway.

She let the door slap closed. "You won't be fine. You don't know how high the surf could get--sometimes houses get washed away. What if there's lightning?"

It felt good, the illusion of motion: one leg stretching, then the other, the ground changing, new places coming, old ones behind. Just as if he'd decided already. Her shout arrested his barefooted step at the edge of the street.

"David!"

She came out of the garage embracing a rolled-up sailcloth: white, with a red stripe. She pressed it into his arms.

He bought a pack of cigarettes, some whiskey and a lighter at a package store on the way to the beach. Not that he smoked, or wanted to drink, but he thought it might bring some false warmth.

Wrapped in the sail, the chair shoved against the hurricane fence in the shelter of the dunes, he managed to light a cigarette. The wind dragged it down to ashes faster than he could inhale.

His shins were streaked with red lines from the sawgrass. His stomach burned from the whiskey. The rain stung his skin.

He awoke to pale light, soaking wet, head pounding, cheek pressed to the ground. Grit filled his mouth; he had to wash it out with salt.

The sail. The wind must have caught it.

He found it half a mile north, one corner buried, one dragged by the water, the third caught rippling in the air. He had to fight all three to get it back.

The sky was walled with cloud, but the storm had gone north. He stuffed down the sail in the seat of the chair and sat on top. His mouth tasted awful. He rinsed it with whiskey, lit a crushed cigarette.

Then Kate was beside him in a sweatshirt, hood up and drawstrings tight, her towel clamped under her arm. Her legs were bare, pocked with goosebumps. Her freckled nose wrinkled. "You survived."

David coughed. "You're swimming *today?* Are you out of your mind?"

"Every day," she said. "You smoke?"

"Once in a while." He stubbed it out. "Thought it might keep me warm."

She picked the butt out of the sand. "If I catch you leaving one of these here, I'll backhand you. Understand?"

"Sorry." He stuffed it into a pocket.

"Have a nightmare again?"

He nodded.

She pulled the sweatshirt off over her head.

He looked away, feeling like he'd seen something he shouldn't.

"Come swimming. You'll feel better."

He rolled his trouser-cuffs past his knees and stepped into an onrushing wave. The water was freezing. It reached up his shins. A wave approached at the brink of crashing. He braced himself, but when it hit the sand beneath him rolled like the deck of a ship, the undertow heaved at his ankles, and he stumbled, windmilling his arms. He caught himself--barely--and fled to the safety of the shore.

Kate was trying to hide her laughter. He leaned over, dizzy, hands to his knees. "How do you stand it?"

"It's all in the way you go in. Test the water first and you'll never make it. Run. Run from the top of the beach, as fast as you can, so there's no way to stop. Hit the wave head-on, before it

breaks. You'll hardly feel it."

"Ha," he said. "Too late."

She ran and dove, slipping into the face of a breaker. She swam straight out, a small, dark head and a trail of foam against the green. She went on and on. He imagined her never turning--just swimming away, out alone across the ocean.

She dove under. The line of foam sank away.

She burst from the waves two strokes from shore and climbed out, breath ragged. "You don't know what you're missing." She put on her sweatshirt and towel, squeezed the water from her hair. "Okay. I'm ready."

"For what?"

"What did you dream?"

He took a breath.

"I was sitting in the chair in our cabin on the *Gray Seal*. The storm was raging. It was dark. I couldn't sleep. There were birds on the wind, black birds with white wings. I could hear the sailors up on deck, calling the captain, over and over. I kept looking at Eleanora, hoping she'd wake up, so I could....

"Then I looked and she was gone.

"I went to the captain's cabin. It was empty. I went up on deck. There was no one at the helm. I tried to get to it, to steer, but the deck kept changing. Every sailor I passed said she was safe in her cabin, asleep. But they hadn't seen the captain. I watched them all get blown off the ship into the storm.

"For a while, I steered. Then I realized they were right. I'd fallen asleep in the chair. She was safe in bed beside me. Which meant we were the last ones left. If I wasn't steering, no one was. The ship was sinking. I had to save her.

"Then the birds were screaming, and water was coming in the portal, and I fell out of the chair."

David shuddered and got up. He might have gone south, but she stopped him. "David! For crying out loud. It's just a dream. It's just a... chair.

"Come on. I'll buy you breakfast."

She'd had to run home for a pair of her father's sandals before the donut shop would allow David in. They sat in a corner. He stared out the window, his hands in his lap, feeling like the biggest asshole the world had ever known.

"I'm throwing a party tonight for my friends," she was saying. "I'd like you to meet them. It might be good for you, you know. If you want, you can always go back to your chair."

"Sure," he said. "Okay."

She'd hung the garden lattices with strings of yellow lights. The painting was propped on a windowsill. The crescent moon gleamed in a cloud-barred sky; a red star clung close to its tip. Inside, trip-hop thrummed from the stereo.

David squatted on the stoop, nursing a glass that once had held cranberry juice and ice. He kept topping off from the flask, until it was more like whiskey and water. People milled about the porch and garden; her friends were bartenders and waitresses, at least until the tourist season's end. They were nice enough.

Kate wore a set of her mother's pearls, a black dress, and flip-flops. Her hair still clung to itself like she'd just emerged from the ocean. She looked the hostess. She wasn't Eleanora.

She sat with three friends at a patio table, legs crossed, drinking wine. The centerpiece was an abandoned bird's nest: dead grass, fishing line and seaweed. An oil lamp rose out of it. They leaned close, faces warm, sharing secrets. Everyone at this party seemed to be. By some trick of the storm's remnant breeze, he heard them.

"Who is he?"

"I met him on the beach."

One of them laughed. Another shook her head.

Silly, stubborn Kate, their faces said. *Still digging washed-up treasures from the sand. Still trying to fix them.*

He thought of the old couple that had passed him on the beach: older than the flood, still holding hands. No doubt they told their great-grandchildren a story: a hundred years ago a girl and a boy met at the ocean. They watched the sailboats pass and fell in love. They still walk to the ocean every day. False fairytales of love the painful truths of which they'd lied about until they forgot them, perpetuating hopes in the hearts of the young for things that could never be. The lifeguard and the girl in the bikini, their idiotic whispers.

Eleanora, naked, skin silken white, fucking another man by the light of the star-dogged moon.

David stood and dropped his glass among the tomatoes. He brushed past Kate and her friends and out of the garden, walking fast. A chair scraped against flagstone. Footsteps closed on him as he walked down the driveway.

In the street, Kate caught him by the arm. Pearls against her throat. "What are you doing?"

"I can't sit here anymore."

"You've made up your mind?"

He blinked. "No."

"You're going back."

"No," he said, too loud. The chatter of the party died away. "But I'm not staying here."

She let go of his arm. "You want to leave, fine. Go sleep it off in your chair."

"I won't fall in love with you, Kate."

Kate clenched her jaw. She made a fist.

The world went black, like the beam from the Nauset Light. The Milky Way shone behind his eyelids. It hurt. Just for a moment, it hurt him worse than Eleanora.

Someone from the party cheered.

The world returned. He wiped his mouth with the back of a hand and walked towards the beach.

From the foot of the wooden stairs he went north. The cold sand scrunched beneath his feet. He made it a hundred strides.

Behind him the driftwood chair cast its shadow across sawgrass-covered dunes.

He ran back, breath burning in his throat. He grabbed the chair by its legs, the sea-smoothed wood like skin against his fingers, so waterlogged and heavy it felt like lifting a human corpse. He gritted his teeth. With a sound that began as a grunt and turned to a howl, he ran the three strides to the water's edge and hurled the chair over the breakers. It bobbed, then disappeared.

David sat in the chair in a tiny rowboat in the dark, with Eleanora at the oars. The hull of the Gray Seal slipped past them to the cries of birds.

"What happened to the captain?"

Eleanora took an ax from the folds of her nightgown. She raised it above her head and swung it down, striking the keel. A crack gaped in the wood. She swung again. The crack became a hole. Black water spouted up. The ax fell through and disappeared. Through the hole in the boat, the dream-ocean drank them down.

It wasn't as cold as the real one. The depths turned green as they descended. Eleanora's lips burned red; her hair in the currents curled like weeds; her skin was alabaster.

At the bed of the sea the captain awaited, pistol in his hand. Fish had eaten away his flesh. His bones were jet-black, patched with mold.

Davidchoked; he awoke in the sand. Beyond the surf the sea rolled smooth as glass. There was no sign of the chair.

He stripped off his clothes. He ran at the water. Icy spray leapt up from the surf at the impact of his feet. He didn't feel it. A breaker reared, its head flecked white. The dawn glowed through its surface. He sucked in breath and dove.

All noise and feeling disappeared. He floated, suspended. He opened his eyes to the salt. He couldn't see the chair or Eleanora.

His head broke free. He breathed. He gazed across the expanse of green-gray where once, perhaps, a pleasure ship had crashed in a spirit gale while its captain dreamed below decks of his own Eleanora.

He looked back at the shore. Kate's easel stood there.

He kicked and pumped his arms and found land underneath him. He clawed his way out and stood dripping.

The *Gray Seal*, the ship, was where it should be--though there was no sign of red hair. She'd blotted out the seal and replaced it with a man: seated, brooding in the chair.

Leading north from the easel, footprints marred the dew-damp sand. The middle toe was a little too long. He saw the track falter, hesitate, turn back, and go on.

Michael J. DeLuca lives in Boston, surrounded by civil war era graveyards and ramshackle taverns as far as the eye can see. He brews beer, bakes bread, hugs trees, builds websites, and is the operator of WeightlessBooks.com, a fledgling indie ebook site. His fiction has appeared in **Beneath Ceaseless Skies, Interfictions, Clockwork Phoenix, Abyss & Apex,** and most recently **Live Free or Undead,** an anthology of New Hampshire-themed pulp horror.

Death of a Soybean

(The Secret of Soy Atomic Fuscia)

by

Michael J. Shell

Herein more than one would-be destroyer of worlds meets his match.

Outside, the new La Salle gleamed—its shining, hulking form waiting for her to rumble its motor to life. Accelerating down the highway, she imagined it to be in the throes of ecstasy. But it would have to wait for its passion (and she, hers). After months of research and test upon test, Agricultural Physics as the world knew it stood on the brink of an amazing discovery. Still, the La Salle haunted her like a demon-lover. She wanted to drive!

"C'mon, Giorgi, let's take ten and go for a spin."

"Spin! Dat's eet! De spin of de protein molecule must match exactly de spin of de proton around de soy-atomic nuclear. Dis will give us de bean!"

"Do you mean the soy-atomic or the sub-atomic?"

"Oh sheet. Dat fuss de whole ting up!"

"I'm sorry, Giorgio," she sighed. She knew how excited he got several times a day when he was sure he had the answer. She just couldn't help shooting his revelations full of holes. "He's such a wimp," she thought. "The only "beeg bean" he's liable to discover is out in the parking lot—that Nazi, bean-looking car of his. Mom's sewing machine sounds heartier than that little pisswagon he drives."

It drove her crazy. No proper man would be caught dead in that thing. But Giorgio was no proper man. He was a genius—a wimpy, faggoty, genius. She'd kill him before she let him discover bean one.

"Fuss it, I can't tink no more. I take dat drive wit choo, but choo no gonna fast-drive, right? No helmet dis time driving, 'kay?"

"Okay, c'mon!"

The parking lot was empty except for her La Salle and Giorgio's "bean." The moon was sharp in the cold, cloudless desert night. She could see Oppenheimer drinking coffee and reading in the guard shack by the gate. "Now there's a man," Maladi thought, "sixteen cylinders and all of them pumping." Tall, thin and wired on the gallons of coffee he drank, his was a motor she could overhaul! But his mind was mush. He once told her he was working on a formula to release energy from atoms—to create little, earth-bound suns. "And do what with them," she'd asked, "grow beans?"

Maladi opened her door and threw the key across the roof to Giorgio. By the time he fumbled his way into the car she could have her skirt hiked up and her bare ass on the cool, leather seat. There was no other way to drive for her, but she'd be damned if she'd let Giorgio find out she didn't wear panties. She actually hated letting him sit in her car.

"So, where we're driving dis time, Mal?   I'm could be goin' for some cappuccino if we weren't in dis damn desert."

"No cappuccino in Los Alamos" she said. Or any other heterosexual place in the universe, she thought.

"Dat's too bad."

As she promised, Maladi left the helmet in the trunk.   The goggles, however, she retrieved from the dash. Giorgio whimpered as she put them on. "I gotta wear the goggles, Giorgio. Sorry." With precision she slid her key into the slot.   It excited her.   The pounding of eight big pistons brought her to a peak. Flicking her foot off the clutch, gravel flew and tires squealed as she slid to the gate and came to a lurching halt at the guard shack. Oppenheimer looked up at her, coffee running down his shirt and pants. He, too, would never get used to her driving.

"Whatcha doin', Oppie," she called out the open window, "trying to discover a pure-caffeine bean?"

Giorgio roared laughter, slapping his knees with his palms. "Dat guy's such a jerk.   He's a musser fussin' night watchman what tinks he's a pissasist! I'm gonna make heem my assistant instead of choo, Mal."

"Don't listen to Giorgio, Oppie. He's just jealous he didn't think up fusion or whatever you call it."

"Fission," Oppenheimer whispered as the La Salle roared off.

Maladi and Giorgio drove through the desert. The goggles Mal wore were essential. She loved to drive with her head out the window and her mouth open wide, deep throating the dry, night air.

"Choo lookin' like a big, red-headed dog when choo're doin' dat, Mal. Choo're lookin' like an impish setter, I'm tinkin'."

"That's Irish setter," she yelled past the screaming wind in her face. "You know, like potatoes. Irish!"

"Dat's eet!   It's like de potato-

The Japanese were about to take Hawaii. Everyone knew this. Everyone was scared.
Everyone but Maladi and Oppenheimer.

atomics. De dirty potato molecule spins to de tune of de soy-atomics and we have de bean!"

Maladi ran the equation through her mind, looking for the fault she always found. She couldn't find one. It wasn't there. Her accelerator foot came off the floor-board and crashed into the brake. Four tons of La Salle spun three-sixties around and around the desert highway. When they finally came to a stop amidst their own dust storm, Giorgio was shrieking in panic. His eyes were wet with tears of fear and he'd pissed himself. "What in de flyin' fuss choo're doin' dat for, Mal? Choo're scarin' dis piss right out of me on my pants!"

Still, her mind fought to find the error in his formula. There simply wasn't one. He was right. He'd discovered the bean. She looked at him, quivering and wet on her leather seat. "Tell me something, Giorgio, are you queer or what?"

"Am I'm queer or what? What kind question choo're assin' me now, when I'm discover de bean?"

Maladi reached across him to the glove box. Inside was a nine-millimeter, German Lugar. Loaded. She opened the box and pulled it out. "I'm asking you if you're queer, Giorgio, because I want to know if I should give you one last fuck-of-your-lifetime before I blow your brains out."

"Maladi, what choo're sayin'? I'm like boys!"

"Good," she said. Three loud bangs later Giorgio was nearly headless and totally dead on the brown, leather seat of her new La Salle. His blood was diluted with his piss. As she sat looking at his pathetic, dead body it dawned on her that he may have shit on her seat as well.

Oppenheimer knew something was wrong when he saw the La Salle creeping down the highway toward his shack. Inside the car, Maladi was thinking, scheming. To her right was a dead genius who'd just given her the secret of soy-atomic fuchsia. Grown Coal. The energy source of the future, now! Soot-faced miners would be replaced by field hands. No more, "when dem cotton balls get rotten." Instead, they'd be picking Maladi's beans.

But what would she do with the dead flit in her car. "At the very least," she thought, "I'm going to need a lot of powerful cleaning fluid to get that mess off my seat." The guard shack was coming up, growing in the distance like the immediacy of her problem. Oppenheimer, it seemed, held her fate. She had a plan.

When she pulled up to the shack, Oppenheimer was to her left, Giorgio's remains being pretty much out of his sight. "Oppie, I've got a problem.

You're good at solving problems. Do you think you can help me?"

Part of Maladi's plan included hiking up her skirt so that Oppenheimer couldn't help but notice she was sitting on her bare ass. But even that view of her exposed lap fed into Oppy's obsession with nuclear fission. The sight of those thighs made him think of explosions—white clapping thunder and the annihilation of fire. It was a double turn-on that chugged his motor into overdrive.

Maladi was crying in his guard shack, now, smoothing her wrinkled skirt down to her knees. Between coughing sips of Oppenheimer's coffee she weaved a tale. "He tried to rape me, Oppie. Before I knew he had my dress up and my panties off. I hit the break, but when we stopped he had a gun. German, like that car he drives. Good God, do you think he was a Nazi?"

"Communist," Oppenheimer whispered.

She crept closer then, pressing against him. "When he put his hand between my legs, when he touched me there," she breathed at him, her face in his face," I took his gun and it came free. I shot and shot and shot. He was dead."

Subtle as a shark eating, she had him in her hand. He was no match for her feminine wiles. Giorgio's lifeless, half gone head bounced to the love/lament rocking of the La Salle...on its springs...from its long back seat.

All the papers carried the news of the Nazi-Communist who'd tried to rape the lady-physicist who'd discovered the bean. Her new assistant, Oppenheimer, was said to be such a genius he could polish her cars and work physics equations in his head at the same time. They were rarely apart.

The war in Europe was nearly over. Soon the Nazi's and Communists would be enslaved to the Capitalist world. It was just a matter of time. But the Imperialist Japanese were another story. The South Pacific was still their oyster, and their greedy little eyes were once again staring down Hawaii. Rumor was they had a bean of their own.

Maladi could care less. She was happy! She was rich! Each day she and Oppenheimer returned to her private research facility. Inside, amidst nuclear accelerators, Fermi reactors and ticking boxes from a man named Geiger, she rebuilt her motors. Buggattis and Mercedes. Rolls and Jaguars. Lincolns. And Oppenheimer shined. He was to car wax what the bean was to the new world order. In the black and white and gray shine of fenders and hoods, he saw equations. And he saw the sun blazing there like death and destruction. He had nothing against the Japanese. He'd never cared for the Nazis, and he could take or leave the Communists. But beyond his waxed fingers he saw an imaginary button he'd be glad to push, just to see that big bang once. He was such a purist. Fire never discriminates.

Every night, after he'd satiated Maladi's almost violent desire, he returned to the facility at Los Alamos. Without malice, his thoughts conveyed to himself one message, "Fuck a bunch of piss ant beans, I want to see it all at once!"

I t was unusual for Maladi to wake up before nine or ten in the morning. After her nightly collision with Oppenheimer she'd roll off him (or, rarely, out from under him) and fall immediately, soundly to sleep. The sleep of the dead. Few things but physics interested Oppenheimer, but the depth of Maladi's sleeping intrigued him. He once sodomized her in her sleep and she never moved. Another time he put her hand, to the wrist, in a pot of warm water. He actually smiled as she peed the bed. No one was there (and awake) to see the smile.

But this night her sleep was troubled. She had taken the bottom position during intercourse and lay there, unmoved, throughout the exercise. She actually forgot she was being fucked. And though she'd closed her eyes afterward, she was not asleep. Instead she was visualizing a great field of soy-atomic beans. The lemon-sized fruits, reddish-gray, dangled in the breeze. In her vision, she was driving a Stutz Bearcat through the field. In the center of it stood Oppenheimer. His hands were clasped together as if he'd caught a butterfly. As she drove closer and closer to him she could see he was about to open his hands and let whatever was in them loose. She could swear light was escaping from between his fingers. Suddenly, when she was nearly upon him, he spread his hands and there appeared a tiny sun. The sun took flight and flew about frantically, touching each bean in the field and igniting it. Soon the entire field was ablaze with the brightly lit beans, each burning hotter than a hundred times its weight in coal. When the Stutz began to melt she sat up. She was sweating profusely. Her mouth was dry. She looked for Oppenheimer in the bed next to her. He was gone.

T he Japanese were about to take Hawaii. Everyone knew this. Everyone was scared. Everyone but Maladi and Oppenheimer. Maladi wasn't afraid because she didn't care. Her mechanical addiction was all-consuming. Oppenheimer was actually happy. Ecstatic. His equations were complete. Soon he would present the allies with a weapon to put an end to the yellow-menace. He had nothing against them, those Japanese, but their lives were a zero in his equations. They just didn't matter. What mattered was the reality behind his formulas. Without the reality they were just paper, and that he could not abide.

He was in the facility, gathering his work to present to the government in the morning. When they understood they would build the device. It was a shoe-in. "Oppie, what are you doing here? I wanted you and you weren't in bed." Oppenheimer turned to see Maladi. She was wearing a trench-coat over her thin, opaque nightgown. He blinked his eyes in greeting. "I couldn't sleep," she continued. "I kept thinking about your little suns."

"Fission," Oppenheimer whispered.

"What are you doing, Oppie? What's all this?" she asked indicating his paperwork.

"Fission," he whispered again.

"It's the little suns, isn't it? You've done it, haven't you?"

He blinked.

"Oppie, we don't need the little suns, we have the beans. All the energy we need and the real sun to grow them with. I want you to come home now and forget all this," she said, going for his formulas.

In a drawer, behind him, was Maladi's German Lugar. He had removed it from the La Salle for safe keeping. His safe keeping. Feminine wiles or no, he knew what she was capable of. Quickly he turned and retrieved it before she could snatch up his work. It felt clammy in his hand as he pointed it at her.

"You know you can't kill me, Oppie. But what's worse for you is, I know you can't. It's okay. Give me the gun and we'll go. I promise I'll leave your little suns alone."

He knew she was lying. When she took a step forward he shot her in the foot. "You son-of-a-bitch," she howled, "that's my clutch foot!" Leaning hard against a table, she came toward him again and he shot her other foot. As she fell, she screamed. "You don't have the balls to kill me, do you? You're as dickless as Giorgio!"

The Lugar was aimed at her gorgeous red head, but he knew as well as she did that he couldn't kill her. It had nothing to do with her beauty, nothing to do with the sex they'd shared. He just couldn't kill anyone. Not in person.

The sound of a gunshot startled him. He knew he hadn't pulled the trigger. As he fell he saw the guard in the doorway with the smoking gun. "Shit," he whispered as he died.

All the papers carried the story about the Communist who'd shot and tried to rape the woman who'd discovered the bean.

What they didn't carry was the story of Oppenheimer's work, which was now in government hands.

Maladi rode her battery powered wheelchair through the facility. Her cars were gone. The place was frantic with scientists and technicians building Oppie's device. All work with soy-atomics was put on hold in deference to his little suns. And even though Maladi was, in show, put in charge of the project, she knew she was a figurehead. After all, they couldn't give the credit to a Communist.

They were all working on what looked like two giant, steel melons with fins. They were nearly complete. One of the scientists saw her coming. Even with her hugely bandaged feet, she was beautiful. "Would you like to name them, Maladi?" he asked her.

For some reason she thought of Giorgio. "Yeah," she sneered, "call them Fat Man and Little Boy."

Southern writer J. Michael Shell is a serious and dedicated artist. At the University of South Carolina (B.A. in English) he studied under the great American poet and novelist James Dickey. Internationally published, Shell's fiction has appeared in the Shirley Jackson Award nominated *Bound For Evil* anthology, the *Panverse Two All Novella Anthology*, Hadley/Rille Books' *Footprints* anthology, *Space and Time* magazine, Spectrum Fantastic Arts Award winning *Polluto* magazine, *Tropic: The Sunday Magazine of the Miami Herald*, and *The Benefactor*, to name just a few. He has also had a novella podcast on *Nil Desperandum*, and *Sniplits--Audio Shorts To Go* has produced one of his stories for MP3 download. Shell's novel, *The Apprentice Journals* is scheduled for release by Dog Horn Publishing sometime in 2012. Though he has been characterized by the anachronistic title "Old Hippie," Shell insists the correct appellation is "Last Hippie."

In Babel
by Alexandra Seidel

In Babel
you could say prayers for a dozen angels
or recite a demon's sermon on every street corner

In Babel
words were scented with rose
and touched your hungry flesh like kisses,
combed you hair with a zephyr's caress

In Babel
where every compliment was hidden in a maze
yet studded with diamonds, and gilded

In Babel
where there was song before dawn
and long long after sunset, where nourishment
was verse and ballad

In Babel
where no head ever rested on a pillow but floated there--
in this city of a thousand promised dreams
and polished visions that were blazing as the pale light
of sun or moon, we found the rivers in our palms

that flowed wild and freer even than
the torrents of words;
from our hands, milk flowed, and wine
the impregnable solace of stone

and on a glittering beam of starlight
shimmering crystal glass: just like a hummingbird's bone
it rang bells and chimes with the echoes
of words, lost or found, but sung forever

About the Issue One poets...

Alexandra Seidel does not believe in either talking swords or pink elephants. In spite of this obvious limitation, she writes prose and poetry, often--though not exclusively--about the fantastical, and occasionally, some of it gets published: *Sybil's Garage, Electric Velocipede, Beyond Centauri, Labyrinth Inhabitant Magazine* and others.

Every once or twice, Alexandra blogs. She is never quite sure about what. Better go see for yourself:

http://tigerinthematchstickbox.blogspot.com/
http://twitter.com/Alexa_Seidel
http://www.facebook.com/alexa.seidel

Bruce Boston is the author of forty-seven books and chapbooks, including the novels *The Guardener's Tale* and *Stained Glass Rain*. His fiction and poetry have appeared in hundreds of publications, most visibly in *Asimov's SF Magazine, Amazing Stories, Weird Tales, Strange Horizons, Realms of Fantasy, Year's Best Fantasy and Horror,* and *The Nebula Awards Showcase,* and received a number of awards, most notably, the Bram Stoker Award, a Pushcart Prize, the *Asimov's* Readers Award, the Rhysling Award, and the Grand Master Award of the Science Fiction Poetry Association.

http://www.bruceboston.com/

And about the artists...

Mari Kurisato says of herself:

I was born to an Ojibwe mother in California in 1977. I've has worked as a teacher, Subway Sandwich Mascot, part time campaign manager, and digital illustrator. I live with my wife, my brand new baby boy born on September 8th and my less brand new cat in Denver Colorado. I consider San Francisco and Tokyo to be my home towns, despite never having been to Japan.

I am not Asian, but I study Japanese Culture, Politics and Nationalism in my spare time, when not hiding from my cat or desperately trying to earn dollars for diapers. Before my baby was born, I was an avid mmo gamer, anime/manga fan, and aspiring novelist. Now all I wants is sleep. And french toast. I'm seeking more illustration work.

She may be found online at:

marikurisato.com
twitter.com/marikurisato
Mari.art.request@gmail.com

M. S. Corley is a freelance illustrator and graphic designer who is strongly influenced by literature and the past. He currently lives in Washington with his wife and cat named Dinah.

You can find him online at:

http://www.mscorley.blogspot.com/
http://www.flickr.com/photos/mscorley/
http://mscorley.deviantart.com/gallery/

The Book of Barnyard Souls

by

Mary J. Daley

Herein, the power of a comforting way...

"Can you count them, Kalee?"

She nodded and stepped away from her father's side to kneel in the straw that held the row of sleeping piglets. In the next pen, the big sow shoved her snout through the gap between boards. Kalee placed a gentle finger on the first piglet. "One," she said, and moved her finger down the row, "two, three, four, five, six, and seven. Seven, Daddy."

"Keep this up and I just might make you my official pig counter."

She giggled and reached for the fifth pig, the only one awake. The piglet squealed, twisting his tubular body, but she held him against her blue dress until he settled. She stroked his tiny head. A sigh softly extended and deflated his sides.

"I wish you wouldn't bring her out here with you, Ben," her mother said, leaning over the side of the pen and picking her up. "Put it down, Kalee."

"Nothing wrong with showing her the newborns." Her father took the piglet from Kalee, placing it back with the others. "It's educational."

"And when she gives them all names, and asks where you've taken them six months from now, what will you tell her?" Her mother smelled of both pantry and garden. Pink lipstick covered her lips. She inspected Kalee and wiped dirt from her dress.

"She'll lose interest once they're too big to hold." Her father stepped into the aisle.

"I hope you're right."

"I'm always right." He leaned in with his strong scent of barn, squishing Kalee between them, and stole the shine from her mother's lips.

Kalee looked again at the newborns. The piglet she had held looked up at her. Since her mother seemed upset that Kalee might give him a name, she decided to stick with his number instead. "Bye, Five," she called, as her mother set her down and led her by the hand from the barn.

For the next several weeks she often snuck down to the barns to visit Five and the others, but by mid-June, her interest began to wane. Five had become too heavy to hold, just as her father predicted, and he was often muddy from his excursions to the outside pen.

But it was only after Kalee received a grey kitten for her fifth birthday that Five faded altogether. He left her thoughts as soon as she opened the box and gathered the pretty kitten against her. The kitten was soft and light, and when she put him down, he bounced and leapt and chased everything from shadow to string. She named him Rain.

—

Before long it was September, and the start of her first school day. Kalee refused to leave her room, holding Rain close, and shaking her head furiously when her mother tried to take the kitten from her.

"You have to go to school, Kalee."

"Why?"

"So you can make friends, learn, and grow up to become someone important."

"But I don't want to be important."

"Everyone wants to be important, Kalee."

—

In the end, she went. She had no choice. And she soon found herself traveling most days, to and from town by school bus. It was often loud on the bus. The children talked and shouted and threw things until the bus driver had to shout in order to quiet them. Kalee often covered her ears, and watched the outside world pass her by, a world of farms and pastures and lines of trees.

During class she sat on the floor, part of a great circle of children that ringed their teacher, Ms. Adams. Ms. Adams read very slowly and showed them cards with letters and words. Kalee enjoyed learning, but she shied from her fellow classmates, never quite knowing how to include herself in their games. She knew how important it was to make friends, because her mother asked her every day after school if she made any. Sometimes Kalee lied and said she was friends with Molly Green. This lie seemed to make her mother happy, and so she made up stories about Molly and her, and told them at dinner. In reality she waited for each school day to hurry up and finish, so she could return home, sit with her mom, play with her kitten, practice her letters, and fall to sleep every night wondering how she would ever make friends.

—

Then Five showed up one night in mid-October. It was on the same evening that her mother exchanged her yellow summer blanket for the heavier purple quilt. She was drifting off to sleep under its comfortable weight when a soft sigh caused her to sit up.

Five stood by her closet, framed somewhat by Kalee's unruly auburn curls that had strayed to the edges of her peripheral vision. She knew it was her pig even though he was now big and creamy with stiff hairs.

Five lifted his snout and sniffed the air before taking a tentative step towards her.

She stared at him, wondering if she should call for her father but Five interrupted her thoughts by speaking.

"If you wouldn't mind, Kalee, might I snuggle up against you like I once did when I was younger? It is just that I had a terrible day and I can't shake the unquiet from my soul."

"You are awfully big for my bed, Five."

"Yes, but I can assure you I weigh no more than your kitten now."

"Okay, come up then."

Five jumped easily onto the purple quilt to lie across Kalee, placing his head against her small chest. Kalee's heart quickened as she put her open hands on the pig's big head, rubbing him at the base of his ears. She sat like that for several moments before saying. "Is this okay? Do you feel better, Five?"

Five nodded and Kalee watched his body rise and fall gently with his sigh. She smiled. And as she held him he left, simply dissolving into the air around her. She ran her fingers along the top of her quilt. A slight indent of pig still lingered but nothing else. Since the encounter hadn't scared her, she didn't wake her parents. Instead she got down off her bed and gathered Rain from the cushioned armchair where he slept, bringing him beneath the blanket with her. She drifted off with the scent of kitten under her nose.

In the morning before the bus arrived she went to the barn where she was greeted only by the big sow. The stall her piglets had occupied was empty and swept clean.

"You are a nervous little thing, aren't you?"

"I come by it naturally. I spent my whole life running from bigger things."

"What happened to the young pigs?" Kalee asked that evening at dinner.

"They were sold." Her father answered. "They grew too big to keep."

Kalee sighed and pushed her plate away. She wished she had remained friends with Five. It might have made him important.

The next night a second pig visited her. It was not one of her father's pigs. He had ears that fell over his eyes, and a brown spot on his back. He kept his head lowered.

"I met Five the other day," the pig said. "We traveled in the big truck together. He mentioned you. That you had a comforting way."

She opened her arms. The pig

jumped up onto her bed and she held him until he too faded away. He was different from her father's pigs and thinking that being remembered was the same as being important, she switched on her light and took out her old letter book that had plenty of blank pages left in it.

On the first clean page she drew a picture of both pigs that had visited her, trying to include their differences.

Under the picture of Five she wrote in large letters 'my pig', and under the second she printed the words, 'big ear pig'. Satisfied that she captured them well on the page, she put her scribbler away and fell asleep.

—

Rain grew into a cat, and began visiting both field and barn on his daily excursions. Her father often praised Rain for being a good mouser and this made Kalee blush with pride for she loved her cat.

So it was grand news to learn one night that Rain also loved her. A mouse, who sat small and grey on her bedpost, gave Kalee this information. Kalee knew straight off that he wasn't a full mouse. He was like the pigs.

"Your cat loves you very much," the mouse said.

"How do you know?"

"Because your cat likes to play a game she calls capture. In between batting me back and forth for a good several minutes, she talked non-stop about you. I had little interest in her chatter at the time, but when she finally ended my torment, I found myself alone and unable to return to my family. It was then that I remember hearing that you had a comforting touch, and I would very much appreciate a little comfort if you have any to spare. Your cat was far from kind and I am very much shaken by the experience." The mouse ran back and forth along her wooden footboard as he spoke.

"I'm sorry, mouse. My dad says it is hard to make a cat mind, and that her job is to keep this farm mice-free as possible. But if I can help at all, please let me." She laid an open palm on her quilt and the little mouse scurried over and up onto it. She laughed. As light as he was his small paws still tickled. She brought it up to her face and stared into its miniscule black eyes. Its nose twitched, its tail moved, it ran up to the tips of her fingers and back down to her wrist. He looked over the edge of her hand and back up into her face again.

"You are a nervous little thing, aren't you?"

"I come by it naturally. I spent my whole life running from bigger things." He shook his body.

With one finger she gently stroked

his fur, from head to hindquarters. She did it several times until the little mouse sighed and lay quietly in her palm.

"You do have a comforting touch," the mouse whispered before fading away.

She reached into her drawer and pulled out her book and drew the mouse below the pigs.

Under the small drawing she printed the words, 'small and nervos'.

—

Spring arrived and when the cherry tree outside her window layered her screen with white blossom, she awoke one night to a room full of lambs. They were all soft wool and innocence, pressed together as if they shared one heart.

She recognized them immediately. They were Mr. Trevor's lambs. Kalee often watched them as the school bus drove past his farm. She had first spotted them weeks ago, when they were only days old, when frost still clung to both field and fence post. She remembered how they trotted and frolicked behind their wide woolen mothers.

"What are you all doing here?" she asked.

"We don't know. We miss our mothers. We were taken from them." One small voice spoke for all of them.

Kalee avoided more questions. She felt a lump in her throat that hurt when she swallowed. She held out her arms. "Maybe it is best you come one at a time."

The first little lamb with a creamy body and black legs leapt with such grace onto her bed that it made Kalee smile. It trotted over and fell to it knees, pressing its face into her pajama top. The smell of new grass and spring rain had Kalee taking in a deep breath and leaning her nose close to the wool.

The lamb slid its back hooves beneath its body and lay quite still against Kalee. Kalee patted and hugged the lamb.

"Is this okay, lamb?" she asked.

The little lamb nodded and closed its eyes and soon it faded away. Each lamb that followed, Kalee tried to remember something special about it. Something that made it stand apart from the others. One had a small black spot in the shape of a crescent moon on its chest, another had a thin black stripe above its left eye, and one was so white, even its small cloven hooves were cream colour. Once they were gone, taking the smell of grass and rain with them, she sighed and looked over at Rain who sat watching the scene on the old armchair.

"They all were so terribly young. Their mothers must be sad."

Rain licked her paw. Kalee pulled out

her book and began to sketch the lambs. She gave each one a name and a description. This activity took her late into the night because there were so many, and she struggled to spell certain words like 'crescent' and 'innocent'. She finally fell to sleep with her crayons spread around her, her book eventually sliding from her bed to lay open on the floor.

At breakfast, her mother looked over the table at her with her lips pressed and her brow knitted. A few days prior Kalee was forced to tell her mom the truth about Molly because Ms. Adams had mentioned to her mom that Kalee kept to herself too much.

"Kalee, you look like you didn't sleep at all?"

Kalee yawned, "I'm making a book, mom."

"What's it about?"

"It's a list of animals. So they can be remembered. So they can be important."

Her mom smiled. "Well although that sounds like a fine idea, no more late nights".

Kalee nodded, hoping that the visits would stop, at least for a while, because it made her sad that some lives were so short, and less important than others. Who, but their mothers, would remember the little lambs that she had placed in her book.

But word of her comforting ways had spread, and the souls of animals from robin to rooster, tomcat to turkey, visited her, and she felt it only fitting to give them the comfort they came for and to include them in her book. Her nights became a contrast to her days. At night she felt alive in the company of dead animals. In daylight she felt unseen by her lively classmates.

When her first year of school ended, her mother and father took her to the water park to celebrate. After a full and tiring day she fell asleep on the long car ride home.

It was the morning sun that woke her. When she opened her eyes, her view was that of a bull's great face. His horn's points rested on either side of her head, one almost pierced her pillow. She pulled the blanket up around her, thankful it wasn't red and asked, "Might you step back, you're scaring me?

He snorted and his big tongue came out to lick the iron ring that hung from his wet snout. He stomped a hoof down on her carpeted floor and took a step back, bumping into her dresser. When he lowered his brown head, the glint of a new day highlighted a rim of pink around his eyes. "Sorry," he mumbled. "But I've been here all night waiting for you to wake."

Kalee sat up and rubbed her eyes. Her heart quickened, wondering if her mom or dad might peek in. She gulped and looked at the huge animal that filled her room. Since he showed patience not to wake her; she felt she owed him patience in return.

"Where did you come from?"

"It's hard to say for sure. I'm a rodeo bull. The circuit takes me everywhere. I was very sought after. My owner always got top dollar for me. You might even call me a celebrity. Maybe you heard of me. My name is Far Flung," he said proudly.

"What happened?"

"Well, you don't get top bull status without showcasing a little, and so I act up sometimes. But the last time I did, I got my darn hoof caught in the chute's gate, and broke my leg trying to wrestle out of it. The pain was as bad as my branding day. Anyway, heavy bull, broken leg, doesn't take a genius to figure what they did next."

"But you were a star. Why didn't they fix you?"

Far Flung lifted his shoulders slightly. "I wasn't that big of a star."

She opened her arms. "Come here."

He stepped up near her and she wrapped her arms around his thick neck. "You did good Far Flung. Maybe there will be cowboys where you're going and you can be a star again."

"If it's my choice, I would prefer a meadow with no fences."

"Oh, I'm sure you'll find that." she kissed him between his wide set eyes and he sighed.

"They were right about you, Kalee. You have a comforting way." He faded but his big nature remained to fill the room long after he was gone.

—

At the start of grade three, Kalee finally decided on a name for her book. She titled it "The Book of Barnyard Souls." It was a big book, consisting of five full scribblers, a pad of construction paper and many sheets of loose leaf. She had tied a piece of baling twine around it to keep it all together. Both her descriptions and portraits of the visiting animals became longer and more detailed. She kept the book beneath her bed.

She continued to have visitors, and she tried to keep their visits just a little longer each time, asking questions about their brief lives so she could tell their stories well. Kalee also became a better artist with all her nights of practice and soon she put aside her wax crayons and coloured markers, preferring the shading capability of drawing pencils.

And now that she had met and conversed with many barnyard souls, she no longer visited the butcher shop with her mother, or walked near the long freezer display cases at the supermarket. And with every soul she met, she felt a little sadder that she was the one they had chosen to make them important, because she was just too shy to show the book to any of her classmates.

Sometime she heard her mother and father whispering about her. That she looked tired, that she was too quiet, that they wished she had friends. Kalee wished the same.

Her parent's concern grew, and thinking they were helping they sent Kalee to camp the following summer. The camp overlooked a beautiful lake that was surrounded by old growth forest.

"It's very hard not to make friends at camp. I know you will make many," her mother said as she kissed her good-bye.

But the only friendships Kalee made were the ones after lights out. The very first night, as she lay on the top bunk, the soul of a black bear climbed the ladder to sit at her feet. She sighed, sat up and pulled out her book and her flashlight. During the nights that followed she met many other wild souls, from sightless moles to porcupine. Even a great bald eagle perched himself in the wooden rafter above her bunk and he spoke in length to her about his life. He told her how much he loved circling high above the land, just knowing sunlight passed through his wingtips

first before falling across the tree tops and lakes. Like the others, she placed his likeness in her book, spending a great deal of time sketching his wings so they folded properly.

When she returned from camp, her parents looked long at her. Her mother started to cry. Her father frowned. Figuring she must have gotten the same rash as the girl on the bus that sat beside her, she ran into the bathroom to look in the mirror. But besides her pale complexion, and the half-moon-shaped darkness beneath her eyes, she looked fine.

Her mother brought her to a doctor anyway. He took a battery of tests, finding nothing. Her mother then took her to Dr. Kim, a psychologist. As Kalee sat on Dr. Kim's comfortable couch one afternoon, she was impressed with the full bookshelves and the many framed certificates on the wall, each one holding Dr. Kim's name. Dr. Kim must be very important, she deduced.

Dr. Kim sat across from her. Kalee tried to look normal. She kept her hands in her lap and both feet together.

"What activities do you like?" Dr. Kim asked.

"I like to draw."

"And what do you draw?"

"Animals."

"What's your favourite animal to draw?"

She paused. This question proved difficult. "I guess mice. They're easy. But I get tired trying to draw birds. It is hard getting feathers right."

"Why is it important to get their features right?"

"So I can tell them apart. So I can remember each one. But it is getting harder and harder because they keep coming, and I don't like leaving anyone out. I just want to make them important."

"And why do you think they wish to be important, Kalee?'

Kalee shrugged and looked again at the certificates that filled Dr. Kim's wall.

The Doctor fell quiet and began to write. When their session was finished, Kalee remained on the couch while Dr. Kim spoke to her mother in hush tones and handed her a prescription.

That night her mother gave Kalee a pill at bedtime.

"What does it do?" Kalee asked.

"It helps you sleep. Dr. Kim thinks you're not sleeping enough."

"No, thank you."

"Kalee it is not up for discussion. Take it."

Kalee took it and slept the entire night without a single soul waking her.

The pills became a regular bedtime routine for the next few months, and her nights that were once so crowded, were now empty and short, with out

even the memory of a pleasant dream to begin each day with. Except for the warmness of her cat curled against her, she never received another visitor.

At first she was relieved to have the burden of providing comfort every night off her shoulders. She was also relieved that she was now able to concentrate more on her schoolwork and had energy left over to join the art club. But although she was now a different child, awake and alert, she remained withdrawn, spending most of her days alone.

Longing for company, alive or dead, one night Kalee spit her pill into her palm as soon as her mother left the room. She sat up and waited, but no one came. She fell asleep near morning, disappointed. It wasn't that she wanted to see animals in need of comfort, but it was the only thing that made her feel important too, and now it was over.

—

She became a tall, slim teenager who hid herself in oversized t-shirts and kept her hair short enough to prevent it from curling. She painted constantly, now preferring oils on large white canvas. But she refused to paint animals or people or even plants, preferring to paint inanimate objects like cameras and lawn chairs and sinks full of dishes. Her art gained local praise and after graduating she was accepted into a prestigious art school. Her parents were proud, but hesitant to see her leave the farm. They thought her melancholy ways might not bode well in the city.

But Kalee found a certain kinship with the city's treeless streets, and so when she finished her studies, she stayed on, renting a small studio loft. She soon made a small income on her paintings.

Her parents came into the city to attend one of her exhibits. She smiled and hugged them close to her. Her mother still smelled of pantry and garden, her dad still held a lingering scent of barn. Afterwards, she made them tea while her mother walked about her apartment trying to rub dry paint from Kalee's cushions and window curtains.

"Mom, what do you think of my latest one." Kalee pointed with the teapot she held towards a field full of light bulbs.

Her mother reached out and tenderly touched the large bulb in the forefront, "I remember you use to draw animals. Wouldn't animals be easier to sell than these? They just seem a tad cold, Kalee."

"Robert Bateman," her father spoke up from where he sat on her small couch, a teacup in his hand. "He painted animals."

Kalee smiled. "Yes, dad, I know."

"He's known world-wide. A very important painter."

Kalee kept to her smile. "That he is."

"When do you think you might get home next, Kalee. We miss you. The cat misses you." her mom interrupted.

"Hopefully soon, Mom."

———

Her mother called her a month later to tell her that Rain died. Kalee spent the entire night waiting up, hoping Rain might visit. It would've been a pleasure to hear what her old cat had to say. But she was once again disappointed.

Kalee remained in the city for years, but she returned home when her parents became of an age that they needed help to maintain the place. Her father no longer kept pigs, and had downsized the garden into a devotion, not a livelihood. As for Kalee she moved her studio into the foyer where the light was good. In the evenings she sat on the porch or played crib with her parents, and her life felt like it had circled around, ending up where it began.

One afternoon, as she searched for her winter boots in the back of her closet, she found, "The Book of Barnyard Souls" wedged between shoeboxes. It had not been touched in many years. She pulled it out, blew off the dust, untied the bindings, and opened the first page to the crude drawing of Five. She smiled and let a tear escape.

She moved through the pages, running a finger over the crescent moon on the little lamb's face, over the big brown eyes of the bear that had been lured into a field by a pile of garbage and shot for sport. She kissed the drawing of Far Flung, and paused on the page that held several kittens. All abandoned to a long ago winter's night. It had been the pleasure of her life to meet them all, and she suddenly felt very fortunate to have had such an opportunity.

Out of all her work, this unseen book of aging pages, crude drawings and child prose, was her greatest, and had trapped most of her heart.

"What you got there?"

She turned. Her father stood in the doorway. It was the first time she noticed how stooped he was, and how he held himself to the left a little, like perhaps his right hip was sore. "Just one of my old drawing books. You up for a game of crib tonight?"

"Thought you would never ask."

She smiled and took the book with her as she left the room, depositing it in the foyer near her canvas. After her parents retired for the night, she opened, "The Book of Barnyard Souls," to Far Flung and began to paint his likeness on a huge, clean square of canvas. She pulled from her paints and her memory all the details she could remember, painting long into the night, and when she finally stopped, her hands cramped, she laughed out loud for she had captured the proud, intelligent beast as fine as if he stood there. This satisfied her so much that it made up for half a lifetime of painting dishtowels and rain gutters. It had even lifted the corners of her melancholy.

She left the house for some air, sitting down on the top step of the porch. It was November and the air was strong with winter's breath. She rubbed her hands together and watched the sky slowly turn peony pink. She looked up as a sparrow landed on the bare branches of their pear tree. It cocked its head and sang straight into a single ray of morning. She smiled and shook her head. How she loved this farm and her parents. Did it really take her an entire lifetime to realize that she had it wrong in her youth? Those sweet beasts that had visited her had just wanted one final moment of warmth. It was never about being immortalized in a book or on canvas.

The door opened and her mother poked her head out. 'Kalee, are you trying to freeze to death?"

'I'll be in a minute. Just enjoying the sunrise."

"Did you paint that bull last night?"

"Yes, I did. Do you like it?"

"I certainly do. He's so life like. You

certainly did the beast proud."

"He was a pretty proud beast to start with mom. But thank you." She turned and looked at her mother. Her mother was smaller now, her hair thinner, her shoulders a bent hanger under her heavy bathrobe, but she still wore the same shade of lipstick she had worn her entire life. Kalee said "You look nice, Mom."

Her mom stood a little straighter, and patted her hair, looking pleased with the compliment.

Kalee smiled. Her mom smiled back and said "You picked a cold morning to enjoy the sunrise, but I'll leave you to it."

She went back inside. Kalee turned back to the sparrow. Its small head hid beneath a wing while the morning sun established its significance in every feather. Kalee couldn't think of a better canvas, a better page, a better moment for the bird than the one it was in. She sent a wish for it to have many more such moments, for all things to have their moments, before rising and going inside to help her mother with breakfast.

Mary J. Daley lives in Toronto, Canada with her husband and two daughters. Her stories have appeared in *Allegory, Electric Spec, Every Day Fiction* and others.
Find her online at:
maryjdaley.wordpress.com

Letters to the Editor

Have comments, suggestions, complaints, or anything else you'd like to say? Let us know. Email editors@fantastique-unfettered.com. Put "Letter to the Editor" in your subject line.

Idea Factory:

Short genre fiction as a whole has failed miserably at representing itself as an Idea Factory when compared to comic books, where we see even the second-rate content tranversing into other creative mediums.

To producers in other mediums, all that is required is to give attribution to use a Fantastique Unfettered story. For indie producers, this could represent a windfall. Derivatives of FU stories, should they ever occur, would only bring greater attention to our writers.

For bigger players, any individual writer can offer an exception on an option to create a derivative work, which would cost the same as any other option on a typically copyrighted work. What does this mean? Well, it's the same situation that Tim Burton is in with his Alice in Wonderland movie. Anyone can still make a derivative of Alice in Wonderland but they cannot make a derivative of Burton's movie. It is an island unto itself. A story optioned via an exception to CC-BY-SA itself remains under the license, but the 'option with exception' allows a derivative work that is not under the license.

If such a fortuitous event comes to pass, the author makes a nice pay day, and via association, with that comes an increasing likelihood that Fantastique Unfettered can pay writers better rates. Our goal is pro rates or better. We're not there yet, but this is the basis on which we hope to build that reality.

Publisher's Note...

Only just yesterday (as of this writing), I got my first look at the all-but-finished version of the first issue of this new magazine. I had read much of its content, and I understood its general direction, but I did not stick my nose into the details of its story selection, editing and design. I purposely tried to stay out of it for two reasons: I have plenty else—maybe too much else—to fill my schedule and, more importantly, I had no doubt that editor Brandon H. Bell would put together a fabulous inaugural issue with little input from me.

Brandon and I have had a terrific collaborative relationship for a while now, resulting in the recently released shared-world anthology The Aether Age and the forthcoming M-Brane "Double." He educated me about Creative Commons and made me a believer in open culture. When he approached me about producing Fantastique Unfettered as a new periodical with a CC philosophy under the umbrella of my little publishing operation, it took me less than a second to say yes because I knew it would be a lovely new zine. While the content of this first issue is, of course, first and foremost an expression of its individual writers' amazing visions, the package as a whole has all over it the loving fingerprints of its editor. The final result is something that I feel very proud to set alongside M-Brane SF and our book projects.

The pride that I feel now in Fantastique Unfettered is perhaps unaccountable since I had little to nothing to do with the actual work of getting it done, but it's there nonetheless, and I think this first issue may mark the beginning of something very important in the near future of speculative fiction.

—Christopher Fletcher, M-Brane Press

(/Kalpa)

A PERIODICAL OF LIBERATED LITERATUR

FANTASTIQUE UNFETTERED
(UNLESS

ISSUE 2 COMING SPRING 2011

M-BRANE PRESS PUBLICATION

www.ingramcontent.com/pod-product-compliance
Lightning Source LLC
Chambersburg PA
CBHW080806120626
46556CB00009B/3244

DEDICATION

This book is dedicated to two men who have been there for my children since the first day they met them.

Maurece (Chops) Robinson aka Uncle Chops
&
Keven Warr (Husband)

Also my children Santhony, Xavier and Jurnee for just being themselves and giving me motivation.
My Bff Brian Turner for everything. Friends for Life

My husband Keven with his unconditional love and support. You are my rock and I love you for it. (SMOOCHES)

I want to thank my family and friends for supporting me during this busy time. All my midday and late night, early mornings.

R.I.P
Monique Jones.
Gone but never forgotten. I miss those conversations.
SCORPIO SISTERS FOR LIFE.

HHD 1

HOLD DOWN SERIES
PART 1

Hold

Him

Down

SHEEM'A